What is a Strebor Quickiez? Years ago, I decided that I wanted to create a series of short, erotic books that would be designed to be read in the span of one day. Thus, the Strebor Quickiez collection was born. Whether a reader takes in the excitement on the way to and from work on public transportation, or during their lunch break and before bedtime, they can get a "quick fix" in the form of a stimulating read.

Designed to be published in collections of three to six titles per season, Strebor Quickiez will be enticing to those who steer away from larger novels and those who do not have the time to commit to spend a longer span of time to take in a good read. The first set includes *The Raw Essentials of Human Sexuality*, *One Taste* and *Head Bangers: An APF Sexcapade*; the follow-up to my wilder successful novel *The Sisters of APF: The Indoctrination of Soror Ride Dick*. Rounding out the collection is a trilogy featuring three women who receive separate invitations to make their respective sexual fantasies come true: *Obsessed*, *Auctioned* and *Disciplined*.

It is my hope and desire that booksellers embrace Strebor Quickiez and promote them to their consumer base. I am convinced that these books can do a heavy volume in sales and, as always, I appreciate the support shown to all of my efforts throughout the eight years.

Blessings,

Zane

ALSO BY D.V. BERNARD

How to Kill Your Boyfriend (In Ten Easy Steps)
Intimate Relations with Strangers
God in the Image of Woman
The Last Dream Before Dawn

Strebor
Quickiez

THE RAW ESSENTIALS OF HUMAN SEXUALITY

A NOVEL

D.V. BERNARD

SBI

STREBOR BOOKS

NEW YORK LONDON TORONTO SYDNEY

Strebor Books
P.O. Box 6505
Largo, MD 20792
http://www.streborbooks.com

© 2009 by D. V. Bernard

ISBN-13   978-1-59309-179-8
ISBN-10   1-59309-179-6
LCCN 2008939022

First Strebor Books trade paperback edition February 2009

Cover design: www.mariondesigns.com
Cover photograph: © Keith Saunders/Marion Designs

10   9   8   7   6   5   4   3   2   1

Manufactured in the United States of America

For information regarding special discounts for bulk purchases,
please contact Simon & Schuster Special Sales at 1-800-456-6798
or business@simonandschuster.com

When they were finished making love, she rolled his exhausted body over, and lay on top of him, staring at him intently. "Will you do it?" she asked him again. "Will you kill my husband?"

Morton was spent from their lovemaking—ready to doze until he could find a likely moment to sneak out of the motel— but when she asked her question, he fixed his eyes on her. Her body, which had only moments ago given him pleasure, now seemed burdensome as she lay on top of him. Her face was only centimeters from his, and he could feel her breath on his perspiration-drenched skin. He had a sudden impulse to push her off—to escape from her and everything she had proposed fifteen minutes ago, before they started making love….

When she first made the proposition, he had allowed his mind to believe it was all a joke: some sick new form of foreplay, perhaps. In a strange way, maybe the proposition had even turned him on while they were in the moment. She had whispered terrible things into his ears: the ease with which he could break the husband's "pencil neck;" the ease with which he could dump the body out in the middle of nowhere, so that it would never be found. In the midst of their sex, the words and scenarios had been a forbidden aphrodisiac; but now that the sex was over, all the terrible fantasies died away, and he saw only the horror of it.

They were lying in the darkness—he looked at her face via the dim light filtering through the motel's curtained windows. Outside the motel, he heard trucks rumbling past on the interstate highway. They were about forty minutes outside of Atlanta, Georgia at a motel where people came to fuck without pretenses. The rooms were rented by the hour; most of the couples arrived in separate cars; and as Morton listened in the silence, he heard them rattling beds in their furtive search for pleasure. The entire thing suddenly seemed sordid to him; and as he lay there, staring up at the wife, he realized he did not like the expression in her eyes. She was beautiful beyond words, but her eyes were like an abyss, ready to devour him. That same look had been in her eyes when she hired him a month ago to spy on her husband. For a while, Morton had allowed himself to believe that look was lust, but he saw now that she was only using him. He was a tool to her: a disposable means to an end. Even their sex was only a way of baiting him into the abyss. Suddenly repulsed, he pushed her off his body.

"…You're a cold bitch," he hissed; he went to get out of the bed, but she held his arm—

"My coldness didn't keep you from enjoying my body."

He turned and stared at her, dumbfounded; after a moment, he shook his head. "You think because you spread your legs for me a couple times I'll be willing to risk twenty-five years to life?" And then, brushing off her hand, "Your stuff wasn't that good." He grabbed his pants from off the floor and began to put them on. His thirty-five-year-old body still reflected the twelve years he had spent in the Marines. The wife, who was twelve years his junior, stared up at him from the bed, her smooth features seeming almost angelic in the darkness. Morton tried not to look at her—as if her beauty would somehow tempt him back into the bed. He moved quickly, in order to be free of her. Once his pants were on, he realized he had not put on his underwear. They were probably entwined in the sheets, and he did not want to dally or turn on the light to search for them. He just wanted to get out of there—

"I can offer you money," the wife ventured from the bed. He had been buttoning up his shirt. He turned to face her again. His voice was low and dangerous:

"What didn't you understand about what I just said? I don't want *anything* to do with this."

"Are you afraid of my husband?" she taunted him. "You see how old and frail he is: you could easily—"

"Stop it! ...I told you we're not having this conversation!" He was breathing heavily, while she lay there calmly, and it annoyed him: seemed like a mark of weakness on his part. He sighed. "I don't care what you do to your husband," he said at last, "—just leave me out of it." Then, as the entire scenario registered in his mind again: "Goddamn, how stupid can you really be? In all the mystery and detective stories you've seen, did you ever see the young, gold-digging wife get away with it?"

"That's where you come in."

He chuckled mordantly. "You mean while I'm rotting in jail, you'll be sunning yourself on your yacht?"

"No—"

He cut her off before she could explain. "I told you before:

I'm *not* talking about this with you." Looking down, he saw he had buttoned his shirt up wrong. He cursed and started unbuttoning. "...Do what the hell you want," he told her again, "but leave me out of it."

"...Okay," she said after a pause. "Will you at least finish your assignment?"

"You mean spying on your old man? I've followed him on three business trips already. He's not cheating on you. He doesn't even rent pornos in the hotel! You're wasting your time and money."

"It's my time and money to waste," the wife responded.

He went to point out it was the husband's money she was wasting; the cruel irony that she was sleeping with the man she had hired to investigate her husband's infidelity was not lost on him. However, at her statement, he merely groaned noncommittally.

"Will you finish the assignment?" she asked again. "—I'll double your fee."

Once again, he stopped and stared at her. The surreal glow from the fluorescent light outside the motel window was cutting across her face. He again saw she was an extraordinarily beautiful woman. Her skin was like creamy chocolate—so soft and fragrant he sometimes worried he would bruise her during their lovemaking: ruin her perfection. She was the kind of woman men had sacrificed themselves for over the centuries. Indeed, she was the kind of woman a man was happy to just be seen with; but once again seeing the ugly expression in her eyes, Morton shook his head.

He had almost allowed himself to be trapped by her; but he was free now, able to see things clearly after weeks of blindness.

In fact, he suddenly felt sorry for her husband. In every way, her husband, Templeton Ferguson IV, had the type of life people were supposed to envy. The old white man had a fortune in the hundreds of millions: his home and possessions were extravagant; his wife was young and stunning. A side of Morton had liked making love to the wife solely because she was Ferguson's wife. The thought of taking something from such a powerful man had turned him on. Also, like most men, Morton had believed his penis had miraculous powers when it came to women. He had allowed himself to believe it was the good dick he had hanging between his legs that had made the wife choose him over a Harvard-educated multimillionaire. He had allowed himself to believe his good dick had compelled the wife to risk her life of wealth and comfort…but he knew now the wife's sex had only been bait for the trap. For a while, he had taken the bait, and swallowed it whole, but he was free now, immune to her spell.

The wife was still lying on the bed, looking up at him intently. Despite everything he had said to her, there was a calm, confident expression on her face; and as he watched her closely, he realized she still believed she could talk him into killing the husband. It was written plainly on her face. Just as he had believed his dick could make her do something impossibly stupid, she believed her pussy could make him throw his life away. He smiled. Now that he had seen her clearly, he felt calm and confident—and vengeful. Both she and her husband had wronged him: the wife had used him; the husband's wealth and power mocked his manhood somehow, making him feel like a petty fool. Remembering the wife's proposal to double his fee, Morton realized that taking more of their money would prove his superiority over them;

indeed, if he played his cards right, he knew he could continue screwing the wife indefinitely. All he had to do was string her along: bait her like she had baited him. Seeing how easy it would be, his smile widened. In fact, his smile was so peculiar that the wife looked at him confusedly; to cover himself, Morton blurted out:

"On second thought, I guess I *can* finish the assignment." He was still smiling.

The wife, too, began to smile, because she allowed herself to believe it would only be a matter of time before she wore down his defenses. "Good," she said at last. And then, throwing off the sheet seductively: "The night is still young. You may as well come back over here and keep me company."

Morton's eyes caressed every delicious curve of her body. He reminded himself to resist her spell, but his dick was stirring in his pants, so he smiled and walked back over to the bed.

ಸಂ♥ಛ

One day after the wife's motel room proposal, Morton was in Orlando, Florida at the hotel where the husband would be staying. For Morton, this was already the most profitable assignment he had ever had. So far, he had collected over $7,000 from the wife. He worked freelance through an agency, which took in all the cases and then doled out assignments to their member detectives. He had seen their ad in the paper the day he got out of the Marines. After a six-week course, he had started his career as a private detective. Most of his clients had been jealous or distrustful spouses who wanted their mates followed. So, when he first met Mrs. Ferguson a month ago, everything had seemed routine. When she started coming on to him, he had thought he hit the jackpot. Even after last night's realizations, he felt as though he were one of the luckiest men on earth. He knew he could keep this going for at least another month, by which time he should have gotten another $15,000 from the wife. This was perfect.

He had caught a morning flight to Orlando, so he could be at the hotel when Mr. Ferguson arrived. He had already checked into the hotel and hired a rental car, which was waiting in the hotel parking lot. He was at the hotel bar now. There was a long mirror behind the bar, which meant he had a good view of the lobby and entrance without actually having to turn around. He looked at his reflection, and was pleased. With the money he had gotten from the wife, he was able to dress much better nowadays. He actually looked dapper in his new designer suit. He had a smooth, light-brown complexion, and what African Americans had come to call "good hair." Growing up in New York City, everyone had assumed he was a Puerto Rican. He had never met his father, and as his mother was dark-skinned with short, coarse hair, he assumed he had gotten his traits from his father. His mother had always been vague about his father. The few times she had talked about him, there had been something inscrutable in her eyes: either love or terror. He had assumed the combination was either the result of abuse or unrequited love or any of the other clichés that produced single, unwed mothers in the black community. At the same time, as none of his childhood friends had had fathers either, he had never gotten into the habit of expecting a father to be around.

The bartender returned with his drink: whiskey "neat." One

of the things he had always loved about drinking was ordering his drink. There was something sexy about getting a bartender's attention and saying, in a suave voice, "Whiskey, neat." It was like James Bond's "Shaken, not stirred." He smiled.

The bartender was an old white man with a muzzle. "Y'all want anything else?" he asked with a thick Southern accent. Despite Morton's good mood, his smile faded away. He had been living in Georgia for two years now, nevertheless, he still had to concentrate when he heard the thickest Southern drawls. Even when he understood them, he was always left with an anxious feeling: an infusion of panic and dread. More likely than not, it had something to do with all the childhood horror stories his mother used to tell him about the South. She had been a superstitious woman; around their house, she had kept various pouches and smelly concoctions to ward off evil spirits and hexes. In spite of the fact that she and her family had moved to New York City during the 1970s, when she was a teenager, she had talked as if she, herself, had been a runaway slave; all her childhood stories had seemed like things from slavery days. The villains had always been slave masters; invariably, the victims had been enslaved—either by the brutal wills of others, or dark magic.

One night, around his sixteenth birthday, he had heard her screaming out in her room. At first, he had thought a robber or rapist had climbed up the fire escape and into her window. He had run into the room with a baseball bat; but by then, his mother had not been screaming anymore. On her face, there had been a terrified scowl—as if she had seen the face of the devil. When he went to shake her and ask her what was wrong, he had seen she was dead. Later, the doctors had said it was a massive heart attack: her heart had literally exploded in her chest.

He had moved in with some relatives, who had been just as superstitious as his mother, but he had sworn he would turn his back on potions and backwardness—and all his mother's insane warnings. Indeed, after high school, when he joined the Marines and was stationed in Georgia, he had seen it as a test of his manhood: a chance to finally shake off all his childish superstitions. Through the Military, he had been stationed all over the world; but when he was discharged from the Marines two years ago, something about the South had called to him. He had never given it much thought. Maybe a side of him had wanted to know his roots. Maybe it had been that he had no particular place to go. Either way, even after two years of working down here as a private detective, a thick Southern drawl still made his skin crawl.

The bartender was still waiting to see if he wanted anything else. "No thanks," Morton replied. After the man left, Morton sighed. His mother was still inside of him—like a genetic predisposition to a disease. He took a sip of his drink, and liked the burning sensation in his throat. In truth, he really did not want to think about his mother right now. He wanted to turn his thoughts to happy things. He remembered the $7,000 of the wife's money he had in the bank. After he was through trailing Ferguson on this business trip, he would have another $10,000 in the bank. Ferguson was always going on business trips, which meant Morton would have guaranteed income for the foreseeable future. His smile returned, and he took another sip of his neat whiskey.

Feeling invigorated, he swiveled on his bar stool and watched the lobby. Most of the people in the hotel seemed to be there to visit Disney World. In the lobby, there were at least a dozen families with those ridiculous Mickey-ear hats. They seemed like some strange cult; the Mickey hats were like demented yarmulkes. Hordes of Disney-hyped kids were rampaging through the hotel lobby like wild dogs; parents were either screaming for them to calm down or slouched on the hotel lobby's couches, worn out. At times like these, Morton was happy he was child-less.

As he was about to take another sip of his drink, the husband came through the door and began to make his way to the reception desk. The old man walked with a stoop; everything about him seemed to droop. His suit, which had perhaps fit him perfectly thirty years ago, was now three sizes too big for his shrunken body. With the heat outside, the man's wrinkled skin seemed to be oozing off his bones—like plastic placed too close to a flame. His thinning hair was matted to his scalp by his sweat, causing his gigantic ears to stick out prominently. The man shuffled up to the desk as if the balls of his feet were in agony. A colorfully attired bellhop followed him, pulling his two bags on a cart. The bellhop, a pimple-faced teenager, was taking pains to go slowly and match the man's miserly pace. There was something farcical about it, and Morton was waiting for the bellhop to lose patience and run the old man over with the cart.

When the old man finally reached the front desk, Morton sat up straighter and smiled: he liked it when his plans worked out. Now, he could just sit back and observe—even though he did not really expect there to be anything worth observing. Templeton Ferguson IV was as boring as they came: a workaholic millionaire, obsessed with aggrandizing his immense wealth. Remembering that he was being paid from the old man's money again enlivened Morton's spirits. He was about to smile again when he looked up and saw a young, beautiful businesswoman was about to walk past him. She was in a red suit, but the length of the skirt seemed more appropriate for a go-go bar than the boardroom. Morton's eyes traveled slowly up her long, shapely legs. She tossed her hair over her shoulders as she walked, and Morton bit his lower lip, moaning, "umm, ummm, *ummmmm*!" as if eating something delicious.

At the sound, the woman looked in his direction. At first, she only looked at him curiously; for a moment, he thought that she would give him a flirtatious smile, but then, all of a sudden, she began to scream!

Morton jumped, causing the whiskey to spill all over him. The woman seemed so terrified that, for a moment, he believed she had to be screaming at someone or something else. He glanced over his shoulder, but there was nothing there. When he looked at her again, she was backing away from him, terrified, almost toppling over a chair. Everyone was looking in their direction now. Instinctively, Morton glanced at Ferguson: the old man was looking directly at him! The woman was still screaming; she tried to take off running, but only tripped on a chair leg and crashed face-first into one of the glass coffee tables. The thing shattered, and the woman lay there as if dead. Morton had not moved in all that time. He forced himself to not look in Ferguson's direction again, but he had no idea what he should *do*. People were going to the woman now, and trying to tend to her: he could not just sit there looking indifferent and out of place. He got up and tried to blend into the crowd. The way the businesswoman was splayed on the ground, Morton could see her panties. They were pink, lacy thongs. He looked away guiltily. Hotel security was rushing up now, telling everyone to stand back. That helped Morton to blend in. However, without being asked, one of the Disney World moms pointed Morton out to hotel security:

"She started screaming at *him*," the woman explained, gesturing to Morton as her toddlers clutched at her shorts.

"Yeah," someone else added. In fact, dozens of people were staring at him now, whispering to one another—

The businesswoman groaned from the ground; everyone looked down at her, and then back at Morton.

"I didn't do anything to her!" he said inanely. "I was sitting there minding my business!" Sweat was beginning to bead on his brow. He felt like a bad criminal. A side of him wanted to make a run for it—just like a bad criminal. "I ain't do *nothing*!" he said again.

Another of the security officers came up to tell everyone the ambulance was on its way. The other officers again tried to get everyone to move on; one of the officers came up to Morton:

"Are you staying in the hotel?"

"Sure—I checked in this morning."

"You have your room key?"

Morton got it out of his pocket, and the security officer noted the number. Morton felt sick. One of the tourists was trying to take a picture of the unconscious woman, but the security officer stepped up to stop him. While the officer told the man to put away the camera, Morton moved on.

He felt slightly lightheaded. Looking around, it occurred to him he had lost sight of the husband. *To hell with it*! he thought to himself. He needed another drink. Looking down, he noticed his clothes were damp from the spilled whiskey. Yet, somehow, he could not bring himself to care. He had to get another drink first. He returned to the bar and ordered vodka. After the bartender put down the drink in front of him, he reached into his pocket and took out a cigarette. He noticed his fingers were shaking, and this disturbed him. He was feeling his pockets for his book of matches when a hand with a lit lighter suddenly appeared in front of his face. The hand was wrinkled, and had huge age spots. He noticed how long and sharp the fingernails were—like claws. The hand had an unidentifiable scent that disturbed him. When Morton looked up, he saw Ferguson smiling at him! ...It took all his willpower not to jump. Instead, he inclined his head a little, to light the end of his cigarette.

"Thanks," he said at last, with the cigarette hanging out of the side of his mouth. His lips were trembling.

The old man sat down on the bar stool beside him; Morton's mind was working frantically, but there was nothing to do but sit there.

"...You smell just like her," Ferguson started. He, too, had a thick Southern accent.

Morton tried not to think about it. In fact, his mind was not thinking much of anything. The only thing he could do was stare at the old man. On the other hand, Ferguson was at ease. He smiled, and took a cigar from a case in his jacket pocket. First, he sniffed it lovingly, then he lit it. There was something almost ritualistic about the entire thing: something dark and paganish—

The man took his first hearty puff of the cigar, squeezing the thing tenderly between his claw-like fingers; Morton stared at the fingers again, cringing, but that brought him back to his senses. He remembered what the man had said; he spoke up

breathlessly, as if he had been holding his breath all that time:
"I smell like *who*?"

"...Like my wife," the man said with an inscrutable expression. When the words registered in Morton's mind, he felt a sudden chill come over him. He felt the panic of a criminal who realized he had been cornered. The old man's eyes were probing—devastating. However, that was when the husband added, "Your girlfriend must use the same perfume as my wife."

Morton stared at him for a few seconds before he allowed himself to be relieved. "...Does she smell like whiskey?" he tried to joke.

"No," the man said with a chuckle, "but I can smell her perfume—even under all that spilled whiskey."

Morton took a long drag of the cigarette then, because he had nothing to say and he needed to *think*. The cigarette tasted horrible, and his face soured.

The husband was still looking at him closely: as if cataloguing every minute detail of his actions. Morton took another deep drag of the cigarette: it tasted so bad he felt nauseous afterward. Seeing Morton's facial expression, Ferguson got another one of his cigars from his pocket and offered it to Morton. "After what just happened," the old man began, "you look as though you can use a good cigar."

"Yeah, thanks," Morton said as he took it, but he only ended up putting the cigar in his whiskey-soaked shirt pocket. As the husband puffed his cigar, Morton found himself staring at the man's fingernails once more—

"What do you think set her off like that?" Ferguson drawled.

"What?" Morton said to buy time.

"The woman who screamed at you: what do you think happened?" As he said it, he turned back to the scene. Hotel security had cordoned off the area, but the woman was still lying prone on the ground, like a corpse; people were still congregating on the fringes, trying to get a look. The sight of the woman brought a shudder to Morton, so he turned back to the bar, and took another long drag of his cigarette. He forced himself not to look up at the mirror behind the bar, which gave a perfect view of the woman's body. He felt lightheaded and sick. "—I always wonder about things like that," the husband continued abruptly, startling Morton. "One moment you're going about your life, thinking you're on top of the world—that you're the master of everything—and then, before you know what's happening to you, you're *fucked*." He smiled weakly here: not an inviting smile, but an ominous one.

"Maybe she got too much sun," Morton attempted to joke again. At this, the old man smiled more broadly, causing his wrinkly face to crease in many improbable and unsavory ways. Morton looked away, and took another drag of his cigarette.

"...I've always hated this goddamn state," Ferguson went on. "My family used to own land down here—in the middle of the swamp. My grandpappy tried to drain it and grow crops on it, but nothing would grow on it but weeds. ...And the draining did not take: within a few years, it was flooded again. That near drove him to bankruptcy. ...When slavery ended, my grandpappy was ruined. He killed himself on that land: went out into the swamp and slit his own throat. Some say he made a deal with the devil to get back his property."

Morton stared at him, disturbed. He remembered his mother's stories—

"My pappy sold that land as soon as my grandpappy died,"

Ferguson continued. "...But I guess Pappy still loved this state, since he used to bring me down here as a kid—for summer vacations. One summer, we were driving down some shit-hole road in the middle of nowhere when we came upon a carnival show. It was a tourist trap in the middle of the swamp. Me and my pappy got out and paid our two bits to see the show. It was an alligator wrestler: a huge man about your age, dressed in a bearskin suit, so that he'd look like some kind of savage. There was a carnival barker there, telling everyone how the bearskin guy had been raised by a lost tribe of Seminoles, and how he had mystical powers over all beasts. He went on and on with this hokum. Of course, it was all a show for the tourist. Even I was loving it. I must have been about eleven at the time—the age when you fall in love with all kinds of sordid, melodramatic shit. ...They had this pen with a huge alligator in it. The bearskin guy jumped over the railing then, and into the pen. The alligator snapped at him, causing everyone to gasp. Little kids grabbed their mother's skirts; mothers turned their eyes away and grabbed their husband's arms. Of course, the wrestler jumped out of the way effortlessly—the way he had thousands of times before. The carnival barker was talking excitedly, but he did not even have to look to narrate what was going on. They had done this show thousands of times. With a lightning quick movement, the bearskin guy was behind the alligator. Soon, he had the alligator's neck wrenched back and the mouth closed. The once mighty beast seemed suddenly broken and weak. In fact, the bearskin guy was able to keep the alligator's mouth closed with his chin. The crowd applauded. Mothers who had before hidden their faces now looked on in awe and relief. And then, in another mighty movement, the bearskin guy pried the alligator's mouth open and held his head between the jaws. People again gasped and clutched one another. The bearskin guy had done it thousands of times…but then, in the blink of an eye, something went wrong. He seemed to lose his balance on the mud. …The insides of alligator mouths are like spring-loaded pressure sensors. As soon as something touches them, they clamp down. The bearskin guy lost his balance and the next thing you know, his neck was inside the alligator's mouth. The creature clamped down and started its death twirl. …That's how alligators rip meat from their victims. They clamp on, and then twirl their bodies, so that the meat is ripped off. The bearskin guy's body looked like a rag doll being tossed around. For the first few seconds, nobody could utter a sound. …And then the guy's head rolled off. It rolled up to me as I stood just beyond the pen's railing. When I looked down at the head, its eyes blinked—some reflex brain action perhaps. That's when everyone started to scream."

The old man sighed at the end of the story, looking melancholy. "That's what I think about every time I visit this goddamn state: how people think they're in control of a situation, but are only waiting around to be fucked."

Morton knew that he should say something, but the only thing he could think to do was look away from the man's probing eyes. Something about the old man's story had touched him, and he felt somehow *tainted*. He instinctively looked away, searching for a way to escape. The woman was still on the ground; people were still congregating on the fringes to get a look at her—even though hotel security had told them to disperse. During the old man's story, Morton had forgotten all about the woman, but seeing her on the ground again only set off new anxieties. The woman was still unconscious, lying prone. When Morton looked back at Ferguson, the same intent, disturbing expression was on the old man's face. The man's eyes were not old man's eyes: they were bright and sharp. Morton felt doomed somehow—

"Are you here on business or pleasure?" the husband drawled before puffing on his cigar.

Morton again noticed the man's nails: how long and sharp they were. It was another off-putting fact. Morton had never been this close to him before. The man had a dry, musky odor—like something long dead that had just been dug up. Morton winced at the thought, and then pretended to cough to cover up the wince. The husband stood up and patted his back. The sensation was like a cold, damp tongue, even though the man's skin did not actually touch him—

Morton had to get away! The next thing he knew, he was thanking the man for the cigar and bidding a hasty retreat. It was the absolute wrong thing to do, but he was through with this game—with this *case*. He was panting. The cigarette in his mouth tasted rancid, so he spit it out, onto the lobby floor. One of the Disney World moms saw this and frowned, but he was fleeing—escaping before it was too late. In his haste, he pushed past some of the people who had gathered on the periphery. The prospect of fresh air compelled him to go outside. He needed to be revived—*cleansed*. He found himself shuffling along, like the old man had shuffled. For an instant, he allowed himself to wonder if Ferguson had known him—if the man's questions had all been part of an elaborate ruse to entrap him. However, the thought opened up nightmare possibilities, so he rushed ahead as if fleeing from his own thoughts. He did not need this at all! He wanted to get back home—leave this god-forsaken place and this assignment behind him. He would call the wife after he felt sane and calm again, and tell her it was over: that he was through with this case. ...Yet, as he headed outside, even these thoughts failed to soothe him. He felt marked somehow—as if no matter where he hid, he would always be within reach of a man who smelled of newly uncovered death....

When he exited the hotel, the heat was stifling. He stood there wheezing for a while. The hotel overlooked a busy high-way; in the distance, there were the skyscrapers of the city center. Morton needed to see something organic and real—something that was not manmade and corrupt. His mind went to his mother. For once, he felt her apprehensions about the South. Ferguson's story had opened his soul to the terror that had always been beneath the surface of his mother's stories. In his mind, Ferguson was suddenly like an old-time slave master. Morton could see him on a plantation in the old days, sitting on his porch, orchestrating the systematic dehumanization of Morton's kin. The image was so vivid that Morton felt his guts tighten—

Something in the sky caught his attention. When he looked into the heavens, he saw what at first seemed like a floating shadow. He stared at it, mesmerized, as it got closer and closer. For five or six seconds he stood transfixed, holding his breath. Eventually, he saw the shadow's movements were birdlike—but it was *huge*: the size of a truck! He blinked a few times, hoping the thing in the sky was only an optical illusion; but the closer it got, the more definite it seemed. Also, something was wrong with the world: even though it was the middle of the morning, everything suddenly seemed dark. Where there had before been the sound of rushing traffic, there was now only stillness; he glanced around, realizing there were no people around him— no Disney World toddlers and their moms; no hotel personnel…

He heard a beating noise: the sound of two immense wings flapping in the wind. His eyes bulged as he stared up at the thing in the sky. …*The shadow bird.* He remembered the story his mother used to tell him, about the demon the slave master sent out to punish and reclaim his escaped slaves. Morton could not move; he doubted he was breathing anymore. Even as the creature drew closer, its body seemed to remain as a shadow— as immense darkness. And then, Morton saw the creature's face. He made out its eyes: two fire-like slits against the darkness. By that time, the creature was upon him. When its huge mouth opened, revealing the infinite darkness within, Morton screamed. He tried to run for his life—*to flee*—but by then it was too late. In one bite, the creature engulfed him; and then, he found himself careening through the infinite darkness. There was no pain, but he felt the darkness digesting him—breaking him down. He tried to scream and break free, but it was too late.

₭♥ℒ

…One second, two seconds, three seconds. That was how long he seemed to be in the darkness before hundreds of stark, terrifying images began to flash before him. He saw slave shacks and whippings and four hundred years of unspeakable brutality. Most of the images flashed in his mind too quickly for him to analyze them individually, but the collective horror of all the images stayed with him. As he was drawing near his limits, the last image appeared. It lingered a little longer than the others—

maybe an entire second. It was a rose bush, bursting with the biggest white blossoms he had ever seen. Yet, the image terrified him, as if he had seen the face of the devil—

Miraculously, the darkness let go of him; instantaneously, he opened his eyes and screamed. ...But when he looked around, what he saw made no sense. He was inside now—in a hotel room that was not his own. It was more posh. He was lying on a king-sized bed. When he looked down, he saw that he was naked. That was when the door to the adjoining room opened, and Ferguson emerged from the suite's dining room. "I was wondering when you were going to wake up," the man said with an expression Morton could not read.

Morton tried to move—to cover his nakedness—but his limbs were like lead—

"Don't try to get up," the husband advised him.

Morton stared at the man, his eyes quailing. "Wha...what happened?" he stammered, looking around again. He remembered the floating shadow: *the shadow bird*—

"Don't worry about that now," the old man tried to reassure him. "I had them bring you to my suite after you collapsed. But you'll be perfectly fine now—I knew how to bring you back." The man had a sponge and an ice bucket in his hands; he came over to the bed then, and started swabbing Morton's bare chest. Morton gasped when the cold sponge touched his flesh—

"You had an elevated temperature," the old man explained, "—I had to get your body's core temperature down."

"—I'm fine now," Morton said, desperately hoping the man would stop nursing him. But the man did not stop. He was swabbing Morton's chest and abdomen with a pleased, far-away expression on his face that made Morton feel sick. Just as the sponge passed over Morton's navel, on its way down to his crotch, something within him rebelled; marshalling his strength, he grabbed the man's hand, stopping its downward progress. "I'm fine!" he said again—a little too forcefully—but his internal panic could not be denied. He would have fought the man off if he had the strength—beaten in his brains, like the wife wanted. He was panting again; the husband smiled, and patted Morton's hand.

"Yes, you'll be fine," the old man said enigmatically.

Morton tried to move again, but he still did not have the strength. He looked toward the windows at that moment, but the blinds were closed. The husband saw where he was looking and smiled.

"I always keep the windows closed and curtained," he revealed. "Even as a kid, I always hated windows—especially at night. I always thought something was looking at me from the darkness. In my bedroom at home, there are no windows—no way for the darkness to get in when I'm sleeping...."

Morton stared at him for a long while. He had to purge the man's story from his mind before he could think straight again. Glancing down, he saw his clothes were on the floor—strewn in various piles, the way they were when he tore them off to be with the wife and his other lovers. Now that he thought about it, his body had the disembodied feeling he usually had after good sex; his crotch felt slightly sore—drained. A side of him had been fighting to keep from acknowledging it. A sense of panic spread over him as he looked up at the old man.

"You're shaking," Ferguson observed. He was still standing there with the sponge in his hand. Morton looked at the thing as if it were a knife. Gnashing his teeth, he forced himself to move! His limbs were still like lead, but he summoned all the power of his body and soul to escape.

"Don't try to get up," the old man told him now, but Morton ignored him. In fact, he pushed him to the side as he lurched over to his clothes. Leaning against the wall, he managed to pull up his undershorts. Yet, by the time he was finished, he knew he did not have the strength to put on the rest of his clothes. The old man was saying something—trying to persuade him to return to bed—but Morton refused to hear. Soon, the rest of his clothes were in his hands. He was stumbling over to the door. The old man was pushed aside again. Morton was panting—exhausted—but he refused to stop: to allow his body to acknowledge its weakness.

Miraculously, he was in the hallway. He was in nothing but his underwear; a middle-aged woman came out of the elevator and gasped. He pushed past her and entered. Luckily, there was no one else in the elevator. He pressed the button for his floor. He was wretched and sick.

He realized he needed something to drink: either water or something stronger. He needed to be cleansed: to be purified of whatever was within him. His mind went to the shadow bird. He shook his head and willed his thoughts to go elsewhere, but when his thoughts gravitated to what the husband might have done to him, he felt suddenly weak. He felt raped—*violated*—but on a spiritual level, not just physical. His body slumped, and he leaned against the wall to maintain his balance—

The elevator door opened onto his floor. Two young men were waiting to get on. They laughed when they saw him. A crude joke was made. Morton did not hear. He lurched out of the elevator, then groped against the walls to get to his room.

There were more people in the hallway. He ignored them—was too overwhelmed by his internal panic to even acknowledge them.

Mercifully, he was soon standing in front of his door. His key was in his pants, and his pants were still in the pile in his hands—along with his other clothes. He fished out the key, then opened the door. Once he was inside, he allowed himself to collapse onto the floor. He lay there as if dead. The coarse carpet irritated his skin, but he did not move for at least five minutes. He saw it was late afternoon: his window was open, and he saw the eerily beautiful sunset. He reasoned he had probably been unconscious for five or six hours. For the first time, he wondered why the hotel had not sent him to a hospital. He suspected the old man had snuck him up to his suite after he collapsed. That was the only thing that made sense. ...But why had the old man done it? Revenge for Morton's adultery? ...Or maybe the old man had gotten some kind of perverted thrill? Morton's mind again flashed with horrific possibilities of what the old man might have done to his unconscious body. He groaned and forced himself to stand. He needed a hot shower. The impulse overcame him suddenly. He needed to be cleansed. ...And maybe a shower would revive him.

He turned on the light. The room was immaculate: white carpet, white sheets on the bed, white curtains. Nevertheless, Morton still felt dirty inside. He stumbled over to the bed and collapsed onto it. Maybe ten seconds later, the phone rang. It was next to the bed, on the nightstand. He stared at it in bewilderment for a moment; but then, realizing the wife was the only one who knew he was there, he grabbed the receiver eagerly.

"Hello!" he said. Somehow, he was desperate to talk to her, but a man's voice answered.

"This is hotel security, sir."

The disappointment made Morton pause for a moment. "...Okay," he said eventually.

"I thought you'd want to know about that incident this afternoon—with the woman who started screaming at you."

Morton practically had to force his mind to return to it. With everything that had happened since then, that incident seemed like something that had happened years ago. "...Is she okay?" he said at last—even though he did not really care.

"Physically, perhaps, but she's had a nervous breakdown."

"Oh. ...What caused it?"

"Who knows? But she kept talking about some kind of creature."

"...A creature?" he whispered, his mind unraveling.

"Yeah," the man said, as if embarrassed, "—she said it was hovering over you, eating your soul."

Morton stared ahead numbly: it was all he could manage.

"...Sir?" the security officer asked after the long silence.

"Yeah," Morton said hoarsely.

"Anyway, I only wanted to let you know everything's fine. Good day." The man hung up the phone, but Morton knew things were not fine. Everything was wrong. ...What had the husband done to him? He tried to think back—to reconstitute the hours of unconsciousness—but nothing came.

Morton grimaced and sat up in the bed, letting his feet fall to the floor. He checked the travel alarm clock on the nightstand: it was almost 7 P.M. now. It was getting dark outside. He decided to call the wife, even though he had no idea what he would say to her. He picked up the phone and dialed her cell phone number. When he was transferred to her voicemail, he cursed and hung up the phone in frustration.

He was weak and hungry. He considered going down to the buffet—or better yet, driving to a real restaurant and eating himself into a stupor. His thoughts returned to the shadow bird, but he only shook his head now. Some people dealt with their fears by becoming rational. He churned the entire thing about in his mind and told himself the incident had been some kind of heat-induced hallucination. He had been overwrought from talking to the husband, and then he had run outside and passed out from the heat and panic. He told himself there was nothing within him—that his life was not being consumed by the darkness. It all made sense—as long as he did not think about it too deeply. He was rushing now—as to keep himself preoccupied. He had thought before about taking a shower, but he was suddenly terrified of being still, as if his fears would catch up to him. He put on the rest of his clothes, then headed outside. As he closed the door behind him, he vowed he would get the hell out of this place tomorrow.

ဆ♥ဩ

He had the groggy feeling people had when they had slept too little or too much. When he exited the hotel, the heat of the outside world was like a brick wall. His steps faltered, and he stood there for a moment, swaying. He was still weak; he considered returning to the hotel and ordering room service, since it probably was not safe to drive in his condition. Yet, he knew he had to get out of the hotel for a while. He had to get away from the husband and *thoughts* of the husband. He tried to take a deep, calming breath, but the hot, humid air refused to enter and replenish his lungs. Somehow, the late afternoon heat was worse than the midday heat; he could smell the asphalt melting. Everywhere, people walked slowly—*tentatively*. ... Morton headed for the rental car. He felt like smoking a cigarette. When he checked his pockets, he found Ferguson's cigar. He threw it away—into a hedge—and groaned.

To get to the rental car, he had to walk around to the back of the hotel, to the parking lot. He was sure there was a more convenient exit, but he had never bothered to ask. The rental car was like a furnace when he opened it—since it had been out in the sun all day. He put on the air conditioner full blast when he sat down. He was adjusting the rearview mirror when he caught sight of his reflection in the dwindling light. There was something unwholesome about his eyes—something that made his breath get caught in his throat. He switched on the ceiling light frantically, so he could look at himself. ...He gasped. He did not know how it was possible, but somehow, it was as if ten years had passed—he looked *old*. His skin was ashen; there were wrinkles where there had never been before, and his hair seemed grayer and thinner!

Someone entered his field of vision, to his left. When Morton glanced in that direction, he saw Ferguson walking toward his own rental car. Suddenly terrified, Morton turned off the ceiling light and crouched down. He could feel his heart thumping in his chest. He looked at the rearview mirror again, but it was now too dark outside for him to discern anything.

When Morton looked back at the old man, he saw three men in dark, baggy clothes appear out of nowhere, as if the night had given birth to them. The men were dressed in the style of teenagers, with baseball caps and sneakers, but something about their movements was unreal. In the blink of an eye, they grabbed the old man. He tried to scream out, but his cry was muffled by a punch to the face. Morton was so stunned that he could not move. Somehow, the old man was trying to fight back. It was pathetic and ridiculous, but he was trying. One of the youths punched the old man in the stomach, and he crumbled to the ground. Another one kicked him in the ribs—

Morton found himself getting out of the car. A strange energy infused him, and he ran to the fight. He was actually running. The energy was like a drug in his system. The old man was trying to get to his feet. One of the thugs was about to kick him in the head when he heard Morton's footsteps. They all turned toward Morton now. Morton prepared himself for battle. He felt the sickly excitement he used to feel back in his war days. He allowed it to free him—to wash away all thoughts and concerns. Soon, he was upon them. He punched the first thug in the face before he could even move. The second thug tried to attack him, but Morton pivoted to the side and chopped the thug in the throat, sending him collapsing to the ground. The third thug was still over the old man, but he turned to Morton now; and as he did so, Morton finally saw his face—

Morton froze, his body and mind short-circuiting on the spot. The face was demonic: upturned nose, fangs and diseased, maggot-infested skin. As the thing advanced, Morton went to scream; but luckily, a car entered the parking lot at that moment. The thing turned to the car, then all three of them fled. Morton stared into the darkness, unable to believe his eyes, because it was as if they had disappeared into the darkness, itself. In a matter of seconds, they were gone. Morton was still standing there frozen. He was panting; his heart was beating so fast it seemed to be humming. In fact, his chest hurt.

The car that had entered the parking lot turned away from them, and went to the other side of the parking lot. The old man was getting up. The movement seemed to break Morton's trance. He walked over to the old man, seeing his nose was bloody.

"Are you okay?" Morton asked. He held the old man's arm, to help him steady himself.

"Young street punks!" the old man cursed, but Morton remembered the face. Those things had not been human. The old man saw his expression, and assumed Morton was concerned for him: "I'm fine," the old man reassured him.

"Maybe I should call the police," Morton suggested, but the old man shook his head:

"Nah, I'm fine—but I could probably use a good stiff drink. Why don't you join me?" he proposed. "It's the least I could do to pay you back."

"You don't owe me anything," Morton said, instinctively wary of being alone with the man.

"Nonsense—I insist. Get into my car," he said as though everything had been decided. Morton was shaking his head, but the old man's hands were on him; the man's voice was insistent, so that soon, Morton was sitting in the old man's luxury car rental. The leather seats were plush—Morton sunk into his, as if the thing were enchanted. Soon, they were driving out of the parking lot. Morton stared ahead, still in a daze.

 conclusion ❤ conclusion

The old man drove like an old man: slowly—as though he could not possibly have a destination in mind. Other cars passed them, honking angrily. Morton glanced over at the old man and saw there was a content, far-off expression on his face. He was about to ask the old man what he was so happy about, but then thought better of it. He went back to staring out of the window. They were driving around downtown Orlando now. Several times, the old man went in circles, so that Morton became convinced he was lost. Eventually, the old man looked over at him:

"Do you know anything about tantric sex?"

Morton looked over at him confusedly. "About what?"

"Tantric sex: an Oriental view of sex. It came out of yoga and Hinduism and so on. ...Men believed they could drain off female energy through sex. They figured the more pleasure they gave a woman, the more of her energy they received."

Morton stared at him. He found himself smiling: "You believe in it?"

"I think there might be some merit to it," he drawled. "...You ever just sit back and observe sex? I don't mean fake porn sex: orchestrated images of how people wished they fucked. I'm talking the raw essentials: the real deal. [Morton was looking at him confusedly, wary of where this entire conversation might lead.] I suggest you look into it when you get the chance," the old man suggested. "The true nature of human sexuality is not what people think."

Morton had been looking on uneasily, but at that comment, he smiled. "What is it then?"

"Sex is the true vehicle of God's power." The old man's face was so earnest that Morton did not know whether to be amused, disturbed or respectful—the way one was supposed to be respectful of all religious views. When Ferguson saw his anxious stare, he smiled. "You would benefit greatly from my wisdom, young buck."

Morton laughed. "What do you think you have to share, old man?" he said playfully.

"I've figured out the raw essentials of human sexuality." The old man's statement was so bombastic that Morton could not help but laugh. Yet, even though the old man smiled, his expression remained earnest.

"…I was thinking about my pappy just now," Ferguson began when Morton's laughter died down. "That's why I asked you if you believed in tantric sex. There was a rumor about him. He was in his nineties and still bedding these young girls: thirteen, fourteen…They said he would drain them—sustain himself with the sex."

Morton laughed uneasily. "You mean like some kind of sex vampire?"

The old man laughed. "I guess that's what you could call it. …My momma died when I was a baby, so it was only my pappy and me. When I was about ten, he had this thirteen-year-old mistress. He got her from another town. He had this little house out back where he took his women. I'd hear those young girls screaming out from the sex. Sometimes, they'd be screaming for an hour. My pappy had him a man-sized appetite," the old man mused with a proud grin. "…Like I was saying, when I was ten, I finally got the nerve to sneak out back and look in the window. My pappy was with that thirteen-year-old I mentioned. Compared to my pappy, she was just a twig: an itty-bitty thing. I hid in the bushes, so I could be right at the window when they started. The first thing he did was strip her—practically ripped off her clothes. Then he had her on that bed. Soon, she was screaming—"

Morton grimaced.

"Don't be so squeamish," the old man said with a laugh. "Anyway, when that girl started screaming, my first thought was that my pappy was too big for her…but it was more than that. My father was on top of her, but I could see her face, since they were lying at an angle to me. And it wasn't as if I was a horny kid taking a peek. While I stood there, it was like being in church: like seeing God's will being done. It scares you to be around that kind of power. You want to shield your eyes from it—like you want to shield your eyes from the sun. …After a while, I swear my pappy's skin seemed to glow with God's power. He seemed energized—stronger, more youthful. Even that young girl seemed amazed by it. We were seeing God's will: bowing down before the altar of His true church—"

The old man laughed when he looked over and saw Morton's expression. "You don't look too good, boy."

"I don't feel well," Morton conceded.

"Well, you should be back in bed. I told you to stay in my room," Ferguson reminded him. "…But I guess if you hadn't been there tonight, those young punks might have done me some harm."

Morton grunted noncommittally. Looking out of the windshield, he saw they were stopping in front of a seedy-looking bar. By the looks of things, they were on the outskirts of town. The old man parked and looked over at him, still smiling:

"A good stiff drink will fix us both up: make us as good as new."

Morton shrugged, and they both exited the car. Morton felt lightheaded as he stood up. He rested against the car for a few seconds, but moved on when the old man looked over at him, since he did not want to talk about how he felt. The bar was a real dive. The lighting was low; the stools and chairs were upholstered with neon-green vinyl, and the entire place smelled of beer, urine and vomit. At this relatively early hour, only a handful of dour men sat at the bar, their faces morose and distant. The old man gestured to a booth, and they sat down. The seat was sticky when they sat, and the tabletop was littered with shelled peanuts. Morton looked around again, then up at the old man, as if to ask him why he would come into such a place.

"This, here, is a real drinking man's bar," Ferguson explained. "Sometimes a man needs to be a man. You go into some of these bars, and it's as if it's some kind of tea party. You come to a place like this, and you can practically smell the manhood."

Morton chuckled. "I definitely smell something."

A waitress in a skimpy outfit came over, but she seemed drained—as if all her life's dreams had already been dashed. She tried to smile—since smiling at men in bars was the way for waitresses to get good tips—but her face remained grim.

The old man ordered two beers. Morton wished he had not come. The bar was depressing. If this place was a true reflection of manhood then they were all doomed.

"Were you ever married?" the old man asked him now.

"No."

"Really? Never had a special woman in your life?"

"Nah, I spent half my life in the Marines."

"That keeps a man from finding a good woman?"

Morton laughed. "Not at all. When the Military sends you all over the world, you find good women everywhere you go."

Ferguson smiled. The waitress came back with the beer. The old man paid her and gave her a fat tip. Her face brightened. When she was gone, he said, "See how easy it was to make her day? In a place like this, everything is simple."

"You like simplicity, huh?"

"Definitely. For an old man like me, nothing is simple—even taking a shit." He laughed, and Morton could not help but join in. Afterward, he drank down half the beer. He was beginning to hope he would have a quick drink and then head back, but the old man called the waitress over and ordered a pitcher of beer. She came eagerly; this time, her smile was genuine.

"She reminds me of my wife," the old man said when she was gone. Morton looked over at him cautiously. The old man continued: "My wife is a real beauty. ...She wasn't more than sixteen the first time I laid eyes on her."

Despite himself, Morton observed: "I guess both you and your daddy liked them young."

The old man laughed out. "It ain't what you think. ...But she was a real beauty. I was dedicating a library in a small town in Alabama. ...Dirt poor town. I paid for the library: all the books, everything. I've been to countless charity ceremonies like that, full of dignitaries and politicians: people who want to be around power. But she was there this time: young and beautiful and full of life. I knew right away she had something special. She had everything I needed." There was a hungry expression on the old man's face; Morton looked away uneasily. In his mind's eye, he saw Ferguson making love to the wife: her smooth, brown skin pressed against the old man's wrinkled, liver-spotted flesh. When he cringed, the old man laughed apologetically. "You must think I'm some old pervert: a depraved old white man, preying on a sweet young black thang."

Morton feigned disinterest: "It's not for me to judge."

The old man smiled at his attempt at diplomacy. Remembering he had her picture in his wallet, he took it out and stretched his hand out across the table. "There she is," Ferguson announced, holding the picture before Morton's eyes. "Tell me if any man with blood flowing through his veins would be able to resist her."

Morton looked at the picture anxiously, then returned to his drink. "She's very beautiful," he said flatly.

The old man laughed in amazement: "You're acting as though I just showed you baby pictures of my ugly brat. *Look*, at her. Look at her *good*, and tell me she ain't perfection." The old man moved the picture closer, so that his scent of death and disease flared in Morton's nostrils—

"She's beautiful, okay," he said, growing more anxious by the second. "What do you want me to say?" he went on. "I'm happy for you, okay? You have a wife any man would love to have. Is that what you wanted me to say?"

The old man sniggered. "I wasn't trying to brag. I only wanted you to understand how I felt when I saw her that first time. She had everything I needed. And in her eyes, there was a hunger."

"A hunger for what?"

"For life. She was perfection, itself. When I saw her that first time, I had the same feeling I had when I saw my pappy with that young girl. My wife was something to be praised. I felt God's energy flowing through her, and I knew I wasn't ready."

Morton wanted to get away from this entire conversation. "Well," he started sarcastically, "I guess everything worked out, since you got her to marry you."

"It would appear that way, but things are not always as they seem." When Morton looked at him confusedly, the old man continued: "What if I told you I've never made love to my wife."

Morton frowned.

The old man laughed again. "It ain't what you're thinking. You see an old man like me and you figure I can't get my rod up no more. As old as I am, you figure my dick ain't good for nothing but keeping my balls warm."

Morton laughed. The old man concluded:

"I may not be a young thoroughbred like you, but I can still get around the racetrack."

"I'm happy for you," he said with a smile. But then, as the old man's words registered in his mind again, he sobered. "Then why haven't you been with your wife?"

"I'm still not ready."

Morton chuckled. "You'd better hurry up, old man, before you run out of time. If your wife means as much to you as you say, seems you'd be with her every chance you got. You almost seem scared of her."

"I *am* scared of her. I ain't afraid to admit it."

Morton frowned, intrigued. "What are you afraid *of*?"

"If you pluck a flower, it dies, and it loses all its beauty."

"What does that have to do with it? She's a woman—not a flower." The beer had loosened Morton up, so that he added, "You've convinced yourself your wife's going to break if you touch her. She ain't a Ming vase that you've gotta worry about smashing. Hiding from her ain't gonna do you any good. You get your value out of a woman by using her: by doing things to her," he said with an insinuating smile.

"What's the longest you ever went without sex?" the old man asked abruptly.

"...I guess when I was in the war: about nine months."

"I've been married for four years and I ain't had sex with her yet."

"Damn, what are you waiting for?"

"Timing is everything. I've got to wait for the right time and conditions."

The entire scenario had Morton laughing again. "What about your wife? She don't mind waiting?"

Ferguson smiled faintly. "Make no mistake about it: I know my wife has her womanly needs. Indeed, I know she has a lover."

It took all Morton's willpower not to leap out of his skin. He forced himself to look over at the man and maintain eye contact. "How'd you know that?"

"Like I said, I've been around the racetrack a few times. I'm aware of what goes on in my own house." He said this last part with a nonchalant wave of his hand, but his eyes were sharp.

Morton felt suddenly sick and weak. He forced himself to talk again: "What are you going to do about your wife?"

"You mean her cheating?"

Morton nodded.

"It really doesn't concern me."

Morton looked at him in bewilderment. "You don't care that another man is taking what's yours?"

"Ah, but that's the thing: he's not taking anything. Maybe he's too stupid to realize he's not ready for my wife either." He was smiling.

Morton shook his head: "I don't understand you at all, old man." Yet, as he said this, he grasped his head: he was feeling weaker and sicker by the second. He felt empty inside—hollowed out. It was as if he were being starved—as if he had not eaten in weeks. He remembered his face in the rearview mirror: how he had looked *old*—

"You don't look so good," the old man said, but there was a strange grin on his face. As Morton stared at it, it occurred to him his vision was getting blurry. That was when his body began to slump; within seconds, everything went black.

∽♥◅

Regaining consciousness was a slow process. In the beginning, he was aware only of noises: jumbled words and the far-off groan of a car engine. Even after Morton opened his eyes, his mind was unable to decode what was going on around him. Everything was blurry and dark—

"Look, he's waking up." It was a woman's voice. Morton tried to focus his eyes, but it was pointless—

"Never mind him," another voice responded to the woman, "—just do what I'm paying you to do." Morton's mind was still sputtering along, but after a few seconds, he realized it was Ferguson's voice! As always, the drawl triggered a rampaging terror within him. Pieces of the previous scene flashed in his mind: talking at the bar; Ferguson grinning as he passed out... He began to panic: something sinister was taking place about him. He felt the certainty in his soul. He willed his eyes to focus. It took as long as a minute, but eventually, he made out a woman's form. She was on top of him, straddling him. Initially, her head seemed monstrously huge and grotesque; but then, as she leaned forward, he saw it was only a wig. He stared at her in his dazed, semi-conscious state. The sensation reminded him of the time when he was sixteen, and some guys on his block tricked him into smoking a PCP-laced joint. His mother had died the previous month. One of his mother's great aunts had taken him in, but the old lady's superstitions and Bible-thumping ways had only driven him to the streets. He had needed something to belong to. Unfortunately for him, the neighborhood hustlers and thugs had been in a malicious mood that day. They had taken him to the local park, and offered him the joint. After a few drags, he had started feeling dizzy. Soon, they had been laughing at him as he lay on the ground, barely able to lift his head. They had kicked him and pissed on him, and rubbed dog shit on him…but when he woke up an hour or so later, besmeared and defiled, he had taken his revenge with a baseball bat. He had beaten the first two into near comas before the police tracked him down. They had found him walking the streets, his clothes still smeared with dog feces and his victims' blood. Finding PCP in his system, they had sent him to a juvenile prison that specialized in drug rehabilitation. There, he had spent two years with heroin addicts and other youths who had committed violent crimes while high. He had joined the Marines right after he was released. Typically, the Military would have rejected an application from a drug felon, but there had been a war on, his drug test had been clean, and the counselors from the rehabilitation center had vouched for his "moral character."

Morton remembered it all as he looked up in a daze and saw the woman straddling him. She was young—maybe eighteen at the most. He had been concentrating on her face, to see if he knew her, but as he glanced down, he saw they were both naked. Her breasts were pert and perfect. He stared at them as if in a trance—

"He's not even hard," the girl protested.

The response was immediate and gruff: "Then put your mouth on him, gal!"

Morton looked to the left for the first time—to where the old man's voice was coming. There was initially only a shadow there; but after a few moments, the old man leaned forward, so that his face was highlighted by the streetlamp outside. It was only then that Morton realized they were all in a car. He and the woman were in the back of Ferguson's luxury rental; the old man was in the front, looking back at them with an eager grin on his face.

"Handle your business, gal," the old man encouraged her; a few seconds later, Morton's body tensed as her warm, wet tongue began manipulating his penis. He looked to see her head bobbing up and down. Her massive wig impeded his view. The old man must have been thinking the same thing, because he wrenched off the wig at that moment. Underneath, her hair was short and boyish—but she seemed like a real person at last. She glanced up at him. In the darkness, he could not see her eyes. For a moment, he thought there might be nothing there but empty sockets. ...But her head was still bobbing up and down. The sloppy sounds of a blowjob had always turned him on. Despite everything, he groaned.

He became aware his penis was fully erect—which was miraculous, since the rest of his body was still numb and lethargic. His body seemed to be fading into the nothingness—disappearing into the surrounding darkness. Somehow, his erect penis anchored him to this plane of existence. All his strength seemed concentrated on his shaft—

"He looks good and stiff now, gal," Ferguson pointed out. The girl seemed lost in performing her sloppy fellatio, because she only moaned her accent. After a few seconds, the old man became exasperated with her, and screamed, "Sit on that god-damn cock, gal! I ain't paying you for no lip action!"

In his dazed state, maybe it was only then Morton realized she was a prostitute. The girl looked up at the old man in annoyance, then she grabbed her purse from off the floor and retrieved a condom. She was about to rip the package open when the old man stopped her:

"Hell, no! For all I'm paying you, you'd better ride him bareback."

"I ain't trying to catch no diseases," the girl protested.

"Then you're in the wrong goddamn profession!" the old man cursed her. When the girl seemed on the verge of reconsidering everything, the old man added: "If he's screwing my own wife, then he's safe enough to screw you."

The girl looked up at him, confused. "You say he's fucking your wife?"

"That's what I said. Now, stop wasting time, and jump up on that dick. I'll throw in an extra five hundred dollars for you."

Talk of money piqued her interest: "Where it at?"

The old man groaned and took out his wallet. He retrieved five crisp hundred dollar bills and handed them to her. She snatched them out of his hand, then held them up to the light outside, apparently making sure they were real. When she was convinced, a wide grin came over her face. Through all this, Morton remained dazed. He did not fully hear the words; and even if he had, he would not have been able to do anything about them.

The girl shoved the bills in her purse, then she zipped it closed, as if she feared the bills would fall out. Next, she straddled Morton once more, and grabbed the base of his penis. She stroked it a few times, to make sure it was still fully erect—

The old man laughed out as he saw the girl was ready. Suddenly jovial, Ferguson reached out and patted Morton on the shoulder, saying, "You're about to experience it now, boy: the raw essentials!"

Morton gasped as the girl impaled herself on his penis. As a Military man, he had had his fair share of prostitutes. His Military career had been a twelve-year sex romp, interspersed with the horror of war and the boredom of being trapped on distant bases with nothing to do. Throughout the world, prostitutes had one motive: to get their johns to reach orgasm quickly, so that they could dispense with them as quickly as possible. A good prostitute did not need more than thirty seconds to a minute. The girl riding Morton had her teeth bared, as if she were a wild animal. The inside of her was warm and tight, and velvety soft. She clenched the muscles of her vagina rhythmically. Morton groaned. He felt the ridges of her inner walls; as she rammed her hips down on him, he felt her cervix stabbing the head of his penis. He groaned again—half in pain and half from the exquisite pleasure.

The old man laughed out. "It won't be too much longer now, boy! I found a nice young, tight one for you, didn't I?"

Morton's eyes darted up. The old man was leering at him, his yellowish teeth highlighted by the streetlamp outside. The sight was ghoulish, but Morton felt the orgasmic pleasure building up in his belly. In the background, the old man's laugh was grating against his nerves. His muscles clenched; where there had before been numbness, he now felt raw, surging power. And then, all at once, he was in the midst of it, shuddering as his seed sprayed the walls of her vagina. On top of him, even the girl was screaming. He looked up at her face then. It was contorted— *monstrous*. After a moment of confusion, he realized the power he had felt coursing through his body was still building. Instead of a post-orgasmic release, there was an explosive escalation of the power. The pleasure was perfect—as if he had reached a new plane of existence. On top of him, the girl was still screaming;

her face, when he saw it, seemed disfigured: mangled. Her body was convulsing now; and as much as he wanted to believe her convulsions came from pleasure, he knew terror when he saw it. She was trying to get away from him; her arms flailed, beating his chest, but it was as if some force were compelling her to continue grinding against his penis. The sight was horrific, but by then the pleasure had escalated to the point where Morton was blissfully unaware of his surroundings. ...Soon, the girl's body began to cave in. Her young, smooth skin began to wrinkle and droop; her eyes lost their luster and her hair began to gray; but through it all, Morton was far away from it all. Indeed, by the time the girl's decaying husk slid from his penis, he was like a god soaring in the heavens.

ഔ ♥ ൚

After many fits and starts, Morton regained consciousness and opened his eyes. He was in his hotel room. The blinds were open; outside the window, the sun was high in the sky. He squinted and glanced at the clock on the nightstand: it was about half past twelve. Yet, before his thoughts could gravitate to how much time had passed and how he had gotten back to the hotel, he was overcome by the same god-like euphoria from the previous night. He inhaled deeply and took stock of his body. He felt amazing! He practically leapt out of bed. He flexed his muscles, liking the way they felt—the tautness of them. He laughed for no reason...but there was a full-length mirror against the side of the far wall; and when he saw it, he frowned. He walked over to it, stunned. Even when he was standing right in front of the mirror, his frown remained. He touched his face, and then his hair, and then his body, as if to check that it was all real. ...Somehow, it was as if he had gone back in time fifteen years. He had not looked or felt this way since he was twenty years old—

He suddenly remembered everything that had happened the night before. The images were brutal—*sickening*. He retreated from the mirror and plopped down on the bed. His skin was crawling. A side of him wanted to believe it was all a dream. He remembered the last image: the girl's lifeless, decaying husk sliding from his body as the old man laughed in the background. He grimaced. It had to be a dream: a *nightmare*. Yet, he was still in the clothes from last night. He inclined his head and sniffed: there was a stale odor of sex, sweat and decay. He shuddered, then looked up at the mirror again, touching his face.

What did it all mean? What had happened last night? Was such a thing even possible? ...It had to be a dream. He got up and started pacing. Something about the silent room unnerved him, so he turned on the television, hoping the background noise would distract him. He turned it to a cable news channel. Yet, even then, his anxieties would not abate. There was a foul taste in his mouth. He cupped his hand and sniffed his breath. It was as if something had died inside of him. He remembered the old man's scent: newly uncovered death. He retreated to the bathroom and brushed his teeth. He stared at his youthful reflection in the bathroom mirror; but by then, his mind was numb. After he brushed his teeth, he smelled his breath again. The odor of death was fainter, but it was still there. He considered the possibility that the scent was in his head—a sensory hallucination. He groaned; seeing the shower in the mirror, he decided to bathe. He stripped off his clothes, then blasted his skin under the cascade of hot water. Yet, even when he was finished, he felt dirty; he sniffed his breath again, grimacing. He toweled off, put on a robe, then returned to the bedroom. His mind was gravitating back to last night when something on the TV caught his attention. A woman's body had been found in a back alley—"a sack of pus and bones," according to the report. The Centers for Disease Control had been called in. According to preliminary investigations, it was as if all the woman's bodily defense mechanisms had given in at once, causing her to die from about sixty different diseases. They were showing the woman's picture now. They had found her driver's license in her purse. Morton froze when he saw it. ...It was the girl from last night! He stumbled over to the bed, and collapsed onto it. Like his legs, his mind refused to work. All it could manage was a chaotic montage: images of the old man laughing and the girl screaming. He felt like taking another shower. His mind returned to the old man's scent; he remembered the man's manicured hands—his long, claw-like fingers—and how the man had laughed at him—

The door opened; when Morton saw Ferguson walking through the doorway, all he could do was stare. There was a smile on the old man's face. He was carrying a bag in his hand. "I see you're up at last," he said, strolling up casually. Morton clamped his eyes shut and opened them slowly, hoping this was all a hallucination. However, the old man was still there; the surrounding world seemed real enough.

The old man glanced at the TV, where the story on the girl was still playing. He chuckled. Then, turning back to Morton, he continued, "I got us some breakfast." He took some cartons of food from the bag, and placed them on the nightstand. He handed Morton a cup of coffee. Morton was still staring at him as if none of this could possibly be happening.

"Drink your coffee, boy," the old man commanded; despite

everything, Morton took a sip. After the initial shock had sub-sided somewhat, he shook he head, as if to break a spell.

"How'd you get in here?" Morton managed to ask.

"How'd I get in here?" the old man said as if surprised by the stupidity of the question. "I have your key, of course. It was in your pocket last night. How'd you think you got back to your hotel room?"

Morton glanced at his reflection in the mirror. His words came out in a whisper: "What happened last night?"

"What happened?" the old man said, exasperated again. "You *ate*, boy!" he said with a laugh. "You got your strength back, don't you? *Look* at yourself," the old man commanded, pointing at the mirror, "you ain't felt so good in years!"

Morton looked again. In fact, he got up and approached the mirror, touching his face once more.

"That's right," the old man encouraged him. "You *ate*, boy, and now you're good and full." The old man was at his back, grinning with his yellowing teeth.

Morton's skin crawled. He turned from the mirror and faced the man. "What did you do to me?"

"It's too late now to play the victim, boy," the old man chastised him. "You deep in it now." Then, remembering something from last night, he began to laugh again. "You sucked that young bitch dry. I ain't never seen nothing like it! You had a man's hunger—just like my pappy—and you took all she had." At this, he threw his head back and laughed, so that Morton could see down his throat.

"Stop laughing!" Morton screamed. "Shut the hell up!"

The old man looked at him sharply: "Is that how you repay me? I gave you back your strength: showed you the path to life. This is how you show your thanks?"

Morton stared at the man, but only groaned in frustration. He had to figure this all out. On the TV, they were replaying the footage from before. The girl's driver's license was on the screen. "...That girl," Morton said, gesturing to the screen, "—what'd you do to her?"

"What did *I* do to her? You're the one who sucked her dry, boy. Stop bullshitting me now," he said, annoyed by Morton's inability to grasp the larger possibilities. "That gal don't have nothing to do with this. I gave you want you needed, boy. You were dying before me. You had a man's hunger, and I gave you what you needed. You're whole now: *perfect*. ...And I took care of everything. The police can't trace her back to us. Everything's perfect."

"What the hell are you talking about?" Morton exploded. "I don't know what your game is."

"Game?" the old man said, outraged. "I gave you *power*, boy. You feel that power in you now. You can see it in the mirror. You don't believe in what you see and feel?"

Morton shook his head: he had to resist everything the old man was saying. He sensed it was now a battle of wills, and that his soul was at stake. "I don't know what you're trying to do to me," he started, "—but I'm not going to jail for what you did to that girl." As he said this last part, he pointed at the TV.

The old man laughed. "Jail? Goddamn, boy, you have no imagination at all! With the power I gave you, you're worrying about jail? Look at yourself, boy," he said, grasping Morton's arm and turning him to the mirror. "Trust what you see."

Morton shook his head. None of this could be happening... but his face was young; his body was strong...he shook his head again—this time helplessly—and turned to the old man. As he did so, he remembered what Ferguson had said to the prostitute last night—about Morton being good enough for her since he was screwing Ferguson's wife. Morton's eyes widened with awareness. "...You're trying to fuck me. Is that it? You're trying to get back at me for what I did to your wife?"

Ferguson laughed dismissively. "Like I told you before, I don't care about my wife's indiscretions."

"Then why are you doing this?" Morton asked, totally lost. "What the hell do you want from me?"

"There is something I would like you to do, but you make my motives sound so mercenary," the old man said, smiling coyly.

"Well, that's the way people are," Morton countered. "When they do something, they expect something back."

"...Fair enough," the old man said with a sigh, rubbing his chin. "I would like you to perform a service for me. I'd like you to kill my wife."

ॐ♥ॐ

Morton retreated a step, then he walked around the man, as if fearful he would be attacked by a rabid dog. It was ridiculous of course, given the old man was so much smaller and frailer than him. Either way, Morton was out of breath. He meandered back to the bed, and sat down, grasping his head in his hands. He tried to figure out how all this could have happened, but his mind was still sputtering along—

"I can tell you exactly where she's going to be," the old man began. "You could make it look like an accident: some kind of street crime."

Morton forced himself to speak, as if the old man's words were poisoning him. "Look, I think you have the wrong man."

"Nonsense," the old man said, smiling confidently. "We both know you're a killer. I checked into your background and know what you did in the war. There was that matter of the men in your unit raping that young girl…killing her and her entire family to cover it up—"

"That had nothing to do with me!" Morton screamed. Even after all these years, the memory and accusation still touched a raw nerve.

"You were the sergeant in charge," the old man said calmly. "You set the tone. All that killing y'all done in that war changes a man, don't it? It makes him hunger for that forbidden fruit. War fills men with the illusion of God's power: you decide who lives and who dies. …It's hard to go from that to a two-bit private eye. You still get to carry a gun, but there are so-called laws over here. Over here, if you're responsible for the murder and rape of a young girl, you get more than a dishonorable discharge." As he said these last words, he gestured over to the television. The blanket coverage of the prostitute's death was still there. Morton grimaced. When the old man saw his cowed expression, he continued, "I'm giving you the opportunity to reclaim the power you're hungering for. No more of this 'rent-a-cop' bullshit. Claim your true power, boy—your rightful position in society. …I've figured out exactly how you could kill my wife—"

Morton instinctively shook his head. "Look, I don't know what you're expecting—"

"I'm expecting you to use the power I gave you, boy. That's what I'm expecting. I *freed* you. I gave you the power! Look at yourself, boy!" the old man said again, pointing to the mirror. "You haven't felt so strong in years. All those little wrinkles and aches are gone now. Your hair is dark and thick again. Let's not play these games with one another. You've tasted power, boy—*God's* power—and you know you're willing to do anything to keep it. Let's not play these games."

Morton looked up at the man helplessly. He did not know if the man was right about him or not, but he felt he had to talk: to speak up before the man's words eroded the last of his soul. "What are you expecting me to do? Just go back to Georgia and gun her down? I ain't no saint, but I'm not—"

The old man shushed him. "For now, I only want you to watch her."

"Watch her?"

"Yeah, just follow her around—observe her for a few days."

"And then what?"

"The rest will take care of itself."

Morton sensed a trap; he stood up and walked away—over to the window, as if he would be able to escape through it. They were on the tenth floor. He could see the highway in the distance: all those little cars zooming past. After a few moments, he turned back to the old man. "Why would you want to kill her anyway? Last night you were telling me how she was everything you needed. You showed me her picture—talked about how beautiful she was—why would you want to kill her?"

The old man scoffed: "Loving a woman is as good a reason to kill her as hating her. It don't make no difference." Then, in response to the disillusioned look on Morton's face: "Just go to her, boy. Watch her a few days. I'm a believer in fate. What will be will be." When Morton still seemed unconvinced, the old man added, "I'll pay you handsomely."

"Handsomely? What does that mean?"

The old man chuckled. "I like that: you get down to practical matters. I'll pay you ten thousand, just to go to her. Then, I'll pay you five more a day to follow her, plus fifty thousand when the deed is complete."

Morton took a deep breath, releasing it slowly. He did not know what he was feeling. Either talk of money had him excited or terrified. He could not tell the difference anymore, and this disturbed him.

"You have nothing to lose," the old man encouraged him. "All you have to do is follow her—observe her for yourself. I'll leave a package for you at the front desk. You can decide for yourself then. If not, it was a pleasure doing business with you." At this, the old man extended his hand for Morton to shake. Morton stared at the long, spindly fingers, willing himself not to shudder. When he took the old man's hand in his, the flesh had the consistency of raw meat. Morton's skin crawled, but the old man was smiling, as if he had seen deep into Morton's soul, and was pleased.

⁞♥⁞

Morton tried to eat some of the food Ferguson had brought, but everything suddenly tasted like straw. He still had the urge to take another shower and brush his teeth—anything to cleanse himself—

The phone began to ring. He jumped, looking at it as if it were a bomb. As the delusion ebbed from his system, he grabbed the receiver.

"Hello?" His voice was tentative.

"It's about time!" It was a woman's voice. Two or three seconds passed before Morton recognized it. It was the wife. The only thing he could do was sit there, staring ahead in shock. "Are you there?" she asked after the silence.

"Yeah," he said, regaining his senses.

"Why isn't your cell phone on?"

The thing was still in his carry-on bag, turned off. In truth, he was not one for modern technology—

"Anyway," the wife moved ahead, "I want you to do something for me." There was an excited edge to her voice.

"What do you want?" he mumbled, wary.

"I got a call from a woman about fifteen minutes ago. She called the house asking for my husband. She said his son was sick."

"His son?" Morton said, his face creasing. He had done a background check on Ferguson, himself. He knew the man had no children. "Are you sure?" he asked at last.

"Of course I'm not sure," she said peevishly. "That's why I need you. The woman was calling from South Florida—some backwater town. If this works out," she said excitedly, "I could use it for a divorce."

Morton groaned. "I'm not sure this is for me."

"What do you mean? You're a private detective, aren't you?"

"Look," he began, feeling worn down, "I'm tired. I just want to get away from both of you."

"'Both of you'?" she said, confused.

He rushed ahead, in order to cover up his gaffe. "I'm tired, that's all. I'm worn out."

She sighed. "Do this for me and you won't have to do anything else. If this works out for me, we'll both be set financially—"

"Goddamnit!" he raged, "stop waving money in front of me! I'm sick of you two!" ...He regretted it the moment the words were out of his mouth.

"...My husband offer you money?" the wife asked after a moment of silence.

"No," Morton lied, "—I just want this to be over."

"...Please do this for me. I'd be grateful to you."

He sighed.

"It'll only take a couple hours. Just drive down there, talk to the woman, see the kid, and check out her story."

"Should I do a DNA test while I'm at it?" he said sarcastically.

She paused. "Please, baby," she begged him; and then, jokingly, "It's not as though I'm asking you to kill anyone this time."

He shook his head, but there was a smile on his lips: "You're something else."

Sensing him waver, she pressed the issue: "Do this for me, baby. I'll be good to you. *Please—*"

"Okay! *Shit,*" he cursed after he had given in.

She was thanking him now, and giving him the woman's information—

"Slow down," he stopped her. "Let me write this down."

She gave him the directions again, and he wrote them down. After he had put down the phone, he felt trapped—doomed. Now, both the husband and the wife were his clients! He shook his head. "Shit!" How had it happened? He tried to think back, but his mind froze up as it reached last night's events. He groaned. Maybe a long drive would help him. Maybe he needed a diversion. Once again, he looked at himself in the mirror. There was no way to make sense of it. More troublingly, the few facts pointed to something too horrific to contemplate. He turned off the TV. He did not want to see any more footage on the girl's death. In the relative silence, he moved quickly. He wondered if he should check out of the hotel now. The wife said the place was a two-hour drive to the south. He would have to come back this way either way, to catch the plane back to Atlanta. After coming back from the wife's wild goose chase (he was still certain Ferguson did not have kids) he would need a hotel room for the night. He would check out after he came back.

He went downstairs. In the lobby, he remembered Ferguson, and what the old man had said about leaving a package. He grimaced. He went to the front desk and asked if a package had been left for him. The desk attendant was a middle-aged gay man with a bad toupee. When the attendant said there was no package, Morton was relieved. He exited the hotel and went to his rental car.

₨♥ℜ

The two-hour drive turned into four hours. The back roads had no street signs; the deeper he went into the swamp, the fewer people there were. The map he bought at a gas station proved useless. Once he got into the deepest recesses of the swamp—where there were unmapped dirt roads—he was on his own.

After driving down a sinewy dirt road for half an hour, he was about to turn back when he came upon a wretched-looking old black man in mud-stained overalls. Apparently the man was a trapper or something, because he had a dead opossum (or some such creature) by the tail. Morton stopped and rolled down the passenger side window to ask for directions. When he began talking, the wretched man looked at him in a slack-jawed way, as if he were talking French. Morton stopped in mid-sentence: "Can you understand me?" he asked.

The wretched man blinked, then frowned: "Who you looking for?"

Morton checked the name he had written down along with the wife's directions. When he said the name, the wretched man practically jumped out of his skin.

"What you want with her!" the man yelled. Then, squinting and scrutinizing Morton's face: "You one of his kin?"

"Who?"

"Ferguson."

This time, it was Morton who jumped. He shook his head—two or three times—as if fighting off something. At last, he said, "No—I'm an investigator. I'm on a case."

The wretched man looked at him suspiciously.

"Do you know where she lives or not?" Morton asked impatiently.

After Morton's rude comment, the wretched man snorted in disgust, as if to say he washed his hands of everything, and began to give instructions. Armed with this new information, Morton set off quickly. He wanted to get this over with, so he could go about his life.

In the final stretch, he only knew the road he needed was supposed to be somewhere on the left, within a two-kilometer corridor. He spent forty minutes driving up and down the corridor, until he spotted a footpath through the swamp. Either he had to walk the remaining distance or he was totally lost. He read the wretched man's directions aloud, twice: this had to be the place.

It was probably about four in the afternoon now. It was getting dark. He wished he had a gun or something to keep him safe, but there was nothing. He wanted to say to hell with everything. He sighed, then turned off the car engine: he had come this far, he may as well investigate. As he sat there, he listened to the ambient noises in the air: the calls of far-off birds and insects. He got out of the car. He grunted: he needed to stretch his legs anyway. There were still about two hours of daylight left. He would walk up the path for fifteen minutes. If he did not find anything, he would walk back and call it a day, and forget about all this. He remembered Ferguson, and the package that was probably waiting for him. He grimaced.

...One thing at a time. For now, he would walk up the path and see what was there. Then, he would see about the rest. As he approached the edge of the road, he saw a heavy stick, and decided to use it as a weapon. He picked it up and entered the path. Trees and bushes were thick on either side of it, so that it was dark the moment he entered. He wavered, but decided to push on. He picked up his pace: the quicker he went, the quicker he could be back out. He reminded himself to check the ground for snakes. He glanced at his watch, and noted the time, so he would know when his fifteen minutes were up. In the back of his mind, he hoped he did not find anything, so that he could turn back and forget about all this—

A bush seemed to move behind him. He heard it rustling. He turned in a panic, ready to fight for his life; when he looked, the bush was shaking slightly...but there was nothing there. He willed himself to move. He was running now. The path was so narrow in some places that he had to go sideways. Even then, bushes scratched him. ...This was madness. Nobody could possibly live up here. Five minutes had passed. He was beginning to think he would only give it another five minutes before he turned back, but then he came upon a fork in the path. He looked down each leg: neither one seemed promising. He was about to turn back when some of the bushes on the leg to his right began to shake. It was as if some monster were trying to force itself through the densely packed bushes. Morton froze. Instinct told him to run, but something else compelled him to wait and get a glimpse of the monster. The stick was still in his hand, but he realized his hands were trembling—

And then, with one mighty surge, the thing was clear of the bushes. It took Morton a few seconds to realize it was human: a black boy, perhaps seven or eight years old. The boy saw him, too, jumping in surprise. The boy was covered in grime—as if he were some kind of wild animal. After Morton came to his senses, he took a step closer; but by then, the boy had seen the stick in his hands. The boy was running now, as if Morton were the monster. The boy was halfway down the path, about to dart around a bend, before Morton realized he should give chase. He dropped the stick and began to run. The kid was like a jack-rabbit, jumping over roots with an agility Morton did not think was possible for a human. Three or four minutes passed like this. Morton's shoes were covered in mud. He slipped a few times; he ripped his shirt on a thorn bush, screaming out as the barbs ripped into his flesh.

There were more forks in the path. It was getting darker. As he followed the boy deeper into the swamp, Morton knew he would never be able to find his way back to the road. He ran faster, since catching the boy was his only option now. He called to the boy, yelling for him to stop, but the kid was terrified. Morton smelled smoke. When he looked up, he saw smoke rising from a chimney. There was a cabin up ahead. The boy was running up to the cabin now. Morton's pace slowed.

As he tried to catch his breath, he remembered the wife had sent him on this insane errand. The wife had said a woman called her, but there were no phone lines out here—no power lines either. It was as if the cabin were something from two hundred years ago: as if Morton had come back in time. …Yet, he had come this far, and the boy was still his only chance of getting back to the road.

He continued walking. There were no lights in the windows. He was wondering if the boy lived out there by himself, but that was when the front door opened, and an old black woman came out. She walked with a tentative stoop. Her skin was wizened, as if she were over one hundred years old. Morton approached with his hands held up, as if to show them he meant no harm. "I was looking for someone," he began, but the woman laughed out when she saw his face:

"Thank Jesus!" It was a joyous statement, as if she had been expecting him. The little boy poked his head out from behind her hip. Despite the grime, he had bright, intelligent-looking eyes. Morton was still panting from the run, but the little boy was breathing calmly. The old woman was moving quickly now. She came out to meet Morton. Before he knew what was going on, she grabbed his arm and pulled him to the cabin. "There ain't no time to lose," she said as she pulled him along.

Morton's mind was light. It was a one-room cabin. The furniture was rustic and handmade. Even though they were deep in the swamp, the inside of the cabin was strangely clean. Morton grimaced when he realized he still had on his mud-covered shoes, but the old woman was pulling him over to a pallet on the floor. When Morton looked, he saw another little boy. This one was about four or five, covered in sores. The kid smelled like death, so that Morton's steps faltered.

The old woman looked back at him imploringly: "Hurry, son, there ain't no time to lose!"

Morton looked down at the boy again. The kid's eyes were closed: he seemed dead. Morton ventured, "Is there a hospital around here?"

"Ain't a hospital he needing," the old woman said, as if annoyed with him for not seeing that. "It's you he need. *Heal* him, son."

"Heal him? I ain't a doctor!" He tried to back away, but she grabbed his hand:

"Just put your hands on him, boy."

"What?"

She smiled almost euphorically. In spite of her advanced age, she had all her teeth. They were white and strong. She was still holding his hand, and something about her was so commanding that he gave in to her will. Soon, the both of them were kneeling before the sick boy, while the boy who had run through the swamp stood looking at them wide-eyed. "Put your hands on him," the old woman said again. She wrenched off the tattered sheet covering the sick boy. There were sores everywhere. The boy had a pair of shorts on: a tattered, smelly-looking rag. Before Morton had time to react, the old woman brought his hand to the sick boy's forehead—

Morton felt an immediate surge of energy, as if he were being electrocuted. He gasped and wrenched his hand away.

"Don't stop, son," the old woman encouraged him. "Don't be scared. Keep going."

Morton stared at her in shock. The entire thing was insane. Morton looked down at the sick boy uneasily, but the old woman's eyes were still imploring him, so he placed his hands on the sick boy once more. His left hand went to the boy's forehead, while the right went to his bony sternum. Instantly, there was the same surge of energy. Morton gasped. It was not exactly painful, but it was disconcerting. Strange colors and shapes began to dance before his eyes. The surge of energy was escalating. When he opened his eyes, he was amazed to see the sick boy's sores drying up. They seemed to evaporate off his skin—

"That's it, son!" the old woman encouraged Morton. Within seconds, all the sick boy's sores were gone. Now, the sick boy was tossing and turning on the pallet, as if in the midst of a bad dream; and then, all at once, his eyes popped open. Morton gasped and raised his hands from the boy. The old woman screamed out in joy and hugged the cured boy. In her celebration, she pushed Morton to the side. He almost fell to the floor, but managed to keep his balance. He stood up. The woman and the healed boy were laughing now. In fact, both boys were hugging her. Morton took a step back, watching them, then he looked at his hands, as if to ask himself what the hell had just happened.

☜ ♥ ☞

Morton was still standing there in shock. Eventually, the old woman pulled herself from the laughing boys, telling them to go and fetch some water for dinner. They ran outside, still giggling. She got up from off the ground with effort. By the time Morton realized he should help her, she was already standing. She laughed at his expression:

"You look like you seen a ghost."

He opened his mouth to respond, but realized he was speechless.

She laughed again. "You acting like you don't know your own power."

He looked at her helplessly: "How'd I do that?"

She frowned at him: "You ain't never healed before?"

"No," he said, losing his calm exterior. Then, as the entire thing registered in his mind again: "What the hell's going on here?"

She shushed him. "You're okay, son. Don't be afraid of the power. That's a good gift: a gift from God. You *blessed*, son."

"Blessed?" he said, lost. "…What happened to me?" He looked at his hands again.

"Mr. Ferguson gave you that power."

Morton shuddered at the name; his mind returned to the things that had happened last night. It was jumbled in his mind now, like a convoluted nightmare. He needed to sit down.

"Mr. Ferguson's always been good to us," the old woman said beatifically. Morton looked at her uneasily.

"Who are you people?" he asked, looking around.

She chuckled and pulled him over to the window. The little boys were returning from a nearby stream with a bucket of water, and she pointed at them: "See them boys yonder?"

"Yeah."

"Them his sons."

Morton looked at her in disbelief: "Ferguson?"

"Yes."

"Ferguson has kids?" he said, still stunned.

The old woman laughed. "Of course he got kids: two or three dozen at least."

"*What*?" Morton shook his head. He had done a thorough background check on the old man. Ferguson was childless. Before he met his wife, he had been a celebrated, lifelong bachelor. Three dozen kids was not something you could hide, but then he looked around the cabin:

"He's hiding you out here—in the middle of nowhere?"

The old woman laughed. "You acting like there's somewhere else we should be. This is our place right here. This is where we belong."

Morton was still frowning: "You know he's rich, right?" he said, glancing about the cabin again, as if to ask why they were living like this.

"Mr. Ferguson's been good to us," she said simply, smiling again.

As Morton watched the old woman, something occurred to him. In the yard, the two boys had started a game of tag (or something with the same general concept). They left the bucket of water in the middle of the yard, and began running about. Morton looked over at the old woman again: "Who's their mother?"

"Oh, they brothers, but they don't have the same mother."

"They related to you?"

"Yeah, they my grandsons."

Morton frowned: "Two of your daughters were with Ferguson?"

"Yeah," she said as if proud.

"Where are they? They live out here, too?"

"No," she said simply. "They dead."

He paused. "Dead?"

"Yes, sir," she went on nonchalantly. "They died birthing Ferguson's kids."

"Oh." He felt he should say something to give his condolences, but the old woman's face remained serene. In fact, there was joy there. Something about it was off-putting. He wondered if she was senile. It was a distinct possibility. "How long have you been living here?" he asked.

"All my life."

Morton nodded his head: a nervous gesture. There was nothing to be said. His attention went back to the boys playing outside. As he watched the cured boy, his mind was pulled in another direction. He looked over at the old woman again: "How'd you know I could heal him?"

She chuckled, as if he had said something stupid. "You got his looks about you, son."

"Whose looks?" he said, lost again.

"Mr. Ferguson's of course." Then, as something registered in her mind, she looked at him with narrowed eyes: "You acting like you don't know he's your daddy."

₭♥ℒ

Morton took a step back. He tried to speak, but his first words got stuck in his throat. "You think I look like him?" he managed to say at last.

"He looked just like you when he was your age." She was smiling in her same serene way; and as much as Morton wanted to clear up the questions in his mind, something about the woman's serenity unnerved him. She and the boys were acting as if nothing out of the ordinary had just happened. He wondered what else they had seen. If he stayed here much longer, he feared they would expose him to horrors he would never be able to withstand—

"I have to go," he said abruptly. He had to get out of there while he still could. He started to leave.

"Already?" she said, stepping into his path. "Why not stay for dinner?" she suggested.

"No," he said too loudly. And then, in a lower voice, "I have to get back before it gets too dark."

"You're welcome to spend the night—since we all kin here."

"I can't." His voice was too loud again, but the thought of being related to these wretched people (and Ferguson) was setting off alarm bells inside of him. He stepped around the old woman and was getting ready to run for his life when he remembered the dark, confusing path through the swamp. He turned back toward the old woman: "Can one of your boys show me the way back to the road?"

"Sure," she said, still chipper. She called to the boys then, and they came running up obediently: *like two dutiful dogs*, Morton thought to himself. She talked to the older boy: "Show your brother the way back to the road."

The younger boy felt left out: "Can I go too, Granny?"

When the old woman said he could, he did a little dance and began skipping ahead.

"It was nice to meet you," Morton said to the old woman, as a way to say goodbye, but she only smiled at him in her serene way, saying:

"Don't worry, son, we'll be seeing one another again, sooner or later." There was a strange sparkle in her eyes; Morton walked away quickly. In fact, he had to resist the urge to run past the two boys ahead of him, and take his chances in the darkening swamp.

As soon as he was back in the rental car, he locked the door. The two boys were still on the side of the road, staring at him. Morton waved at them, but they did not wave back. On the walk down to the car, they had said nothing to him. Morton looked at their faces in the twilight. The younger boy seemed shy. He stood next to his brother in the fidgety way of little children. However, his brother had old man's eyes—as if worn down by life's daily struggles. Morton stared at his eyes for a few moments, as if to reconcile the contradiction; but at last, he shook his head. He only wanted to get away from these wretched people. He remembered the things the old lady had said to him. Did he dare believe those two little boys were his brothers—and that the old man was their father? ...*God*, now that he thought about it, the older boy looked exactly the way he did at that age. Morton's mind went to Ferguson. If the old man was his father, then all of this was a trap. He considered everything that had happened since the old man started talking to him at the hotel bar. He remembered how he had cured the little boy: how he had felt the power of the gods flowing through his hands—

Morton shuddered. He was sure he was going to be sick. He had to get away from this place. He wished there were a way he could forget everything he had learned and seen. The two little boys were still staring at him from the side of the road, like grim scarecrows. He had to get away. He started up the car and pressed on the accelerator. He made a quick U-turn, so he could head back the way he had come. When he had the car turned around, the little boys were gone. He felt alone—isolated in the middle of a nowhere place. Then, he suddenly became aware there was something in the air—a sound that filled him with panic even before he realized what it was. It was the flapping wings he had heard back at the hotel: *the shadow bird*. He stamped down on the accelerator! The bird seemed to be right over him: the flapping was so loud it shook his insides. He kept looking in the rearview mirror, but it was now so dark outside that the shadow could be anywhere. He was trapped in the darkness. He turned on the headlights. He was not a religious man, but he began to pray. He remembered one of the incantations his mother used to say around the house, to ward off evil. He was a believer now. He had seen horrors, and now he believed. In fact, he was shouting the incantation now; he stamped the gas pedal to the floor—

Five minutes had passed. As he listened, he realized he could not hear the flapping wings anymore. Had the incantation scared the bird away? In truth, his heart was beating so loudly that he could not hear any other sounds. He stomped on the gas pedal again. The only thing he trusted was speed…but then a nightmare thought went through his mind: what if he was stuck in the swamp? What if he was only driving in circles, and would always be trapped in here? Now that he looked up at the sky, the darkness seemed too deep. There were no stars—no sign that there might be an actual world out there. He was trembling.

By the time he finally reached a paved road, his mind was on the verge of collapse. He had to execute a ninety-degree left turn when he reached the road; but at the speed he was going, he almost flew into the ditch at the side of the road. The car went into a skid. He barely managed to stabilize the vehicle before it crashed. However, even then, he did not stop. He was like a miner trapped deep in the bowels of a cave. He sensed the foul, poisoned air around him, and knew the only way to save himself was to get back to the surface and cleanse his lungs. He stomped on the accelerator once again.

ಐ ♥ ೞ

Morton relaxed somewhat when he began to come upon other cars. It was a sign the swamp was behind him. He said his mother's incantations again: it could not hurt at this point. He felt closer to her than he had ever been while she was alive. As much as the thought set off alarm bells inside of him, it was true. He wished he had listened to her. He tried reconstructing the things she used to say to him, but he had only pretended to listen to her. Most of her warnings were jumbled in his head. He felt suddenly sorrowful about their relationship. She had tried to keep him safe, but he had bungled himself into hell.

When he made it back to the highway, he felt marginally better. Most of his panic had come from being isolated in the swamp. There had been some kind of primal fear there, which he did not want to consider too deeply. The old woman had told him they would be seeing one another sooner or later, but there was no way he was ever going back there. Nothing in heaven or earth (or hell, for that matter) would ever convince him to go back there again. ...Could Ferguson be his father? He had been asking the same question continually. One moment, he told himself it was impossible; the next, he felt the certainty within himself. ...He had to get his mind away from all of this. He considered going to a bar and having a few beers, but thoughts of bars reminded him of how the old man had taken him to that dive. For a moment, his thoughts went to sex, but then he remembered the wife, and the prostitute, and all the horrors that seemed to lurk behind them both.

Eventually, it occurred to him the wife would be expecting a report on what had happened in the swamp. What was he to tell her? He was barely able to grasp what he had seen with his own eyes: he knew he would never be able to convince her. Indeed, he pitied her for her ignorance and blindness. Ferguson's money had blinded her; she put too much faith in the power of her sexuality and the easy manipulability of men. In her ignorance, she had no idea of the danger she was in. She was concerned with potential alimony payments, when her soul was hanging by a thread. He considered warning her: telling her to flee while she still could. For a few moments, he tried to come up with the words that would make her understand, but he realized she would only think him insane. Even he hardly believed it. ...He sighed.

℠♥℟

He was now driving the last block to the Orlando hotel. Like an overused appliance, his mind had overheated and fizzled out. He stared ahead in a daze. He drove more by instinct than with any true awareness. Only when he had parked in the back of the hotel, and gotten out of his rental car, did he notice the police cars and ambulances on the other side of the lot; but even then, he could not conjure the normal human curiosity. People had gathered on the periphery of the lot, to see what had happened. The police were telling them to disburse; but like dumb beasts, they kept coming and craning their necks to see what had happened. Morton glanced in that direction. A body was lying in a parking space, covered in a bloody sheet.

Even then, whatever curiosity he would normally have had was blunted by the experiences of the last few days and hours. He began walking back to the hotel room. When he came upon the crowd of curious bystanders, he pushed past them rudely. In his dazed state, he was only vaguely aware that they were there.

Eventually, he entered the hotel lobby. The air conditioner was on high. He shivered. Maybe it was only then that he realized how hot it had been outside. His clothes were soaked with sweat. He would take a long shower when he got back to his room. He headed for the elevator. A young couple got in with him. They looked as though they were on their honeymoon, because they could not keep their hands off one another. As soon as the door closed, they began giggling at one of those internal jokes that only lovers had. Morton glared at them until they looked at him anxiously and stopped giggling. Being a big, imposing black man sometimes had its benefits.

When the elevator reached his floor, he exited it in the same lifeless way he had entered. It occurred to him he had not really eaten that day. Strangely enough, he did not know if he was hungry or not. He felt disembodied—separated from his body and the outside world. As he walked, he could not feel the ground. He literally had to look down to make sure he was still walking on the floor.

At last, he entered his hotel room. He hoped he would sleep. It was not that he was tired: he merely wanted to be unconscious for a while. He instinctively knew his body needed time to recalibrate itself. He had thought before about a shower, but he suddenly could not be bothered. He did not even have the energy to bend over and untie his shoelaces, so he took off his shoes by stepping on their heels and kicking them off. After that, he threw himself at the bed. The maid had changed the sheets, and everything was clean and fresh. For an instant, he considered turning on the TV, so the white noise would help drown out his thoughts, but fearing there would be more stories on the prostitute from last night, he decided against it. He closed his eyes.

80 ♥ 03

He was not sure if he slept or not. When he closed his eyes, he saw the same nightmare images he had been seeing all day. Someone knocked on the door, and he opened his eyes. The LCD alarm clock on the nightstand said it was 10:37 P.M., but Morton had no idea when he had gone to bed. All of it was a blur—

A man called from outside the door. The door was knocked on again—louder. Morton sat up and looked about confusedly. When the man on the other side of the door banged the door once more—this time with obvious impatience and anger— Morton forced himself to get out of bed.

He was giddy when he stood up; he fell back to the bed, clamping his eyes shut to stop the room from swirling before his eyes. The man on the other side of the door banged it again—

"I'm coming, goddamnit!" Morton screamed. Yet, he lay on the bed, taking deep breaths to clear his head. He turned on the light on the nightstand, cringing from the glare. He cursed. After five or six breaths, he stood up again. He was still dizzy, but he could hear the man grumbling at the door; and fearing the man would bang the door again, he moved as quickly as he could manage.

When he opened the door, four men were standing there: two uniformed police officers and two plain-clothed detectives in bad suits. He knew they were detectives because they shoved their badges in his face. The motion was an aggressive one, and Morton stepped back.

"Charles Morton?" began the detective in front. He was a middle-aged white man with a bad comb-over and man boobs. The other detective was a heavyset black man around the same age, with a lopsided Afro.

When Morton's heartbeat had stabilized, and the detective's question finally registered in his mind, he nodded.

"Can we come in?" the detective with the lopsided Afro asked, even though they had all entered the room by then. They had stormed into the room after Morton backed away; Morton had stood by the door, watching them helplessly.

After glancing about the room for a few seconds, the two detectives turned to Morton; the two uniformed officers continued to look around. One of the uniformed officers went to check the bathroom. When the man turned on the light, Morton finally came to his senses.

"What's this about?" he said at last.

"We're conducting a homicide investigation," the detective with the bad comb-over said. His tone was naturally bellicose and overbearing—

"A *what*?" Morton said, his voice suddenly hoarse.

"Do you know Templeton Ferguson?"

"Sure, but what—"

"He's *dead*," the detective with the lopsided Afro announced. Morton stared at him for a few seconds. "He's *what*?"

"He was murdered about two hours ago." This was the detective with the bad comb-over. Morton stared at him as if doing so would help him to make sense of all this. It did not; then, when everything came together in his mind, he shook his head.

"You think *I* did it?" he said, his eyes wide as he looked from one detective to the other. "I've been gone all day!"

Both detectives smiled and glanced at one another. "What's your alibi?" the one with the lopsided Afro started.

"I went on an errand." As Morton said these words, he remembered the wife: her proposition that he kill Ferguson. His guts knotted themselves! He could not use his errand to the swamp as an alibi. If Ferguson was dead, he had to disavow any knowledge of knowing the wife—in case she had done it. It was him against her now: her word against his. Maybe she had sent him on that errand so he would not have an alibi. She had trapped him—

The detective with the bad comb-over laughed. "Relax, you're not exactly a suspect."

"Not exactly?" Morton looked at him confusedly, not sure whether to be relieved or alarmed.

"We know some thugs did it," the one with the lopsided Afro explained. "We got the entire thing on the hotel's security cameras."

All at once, Morton remembered the scene from the parking lot: police cars and ambulances and the crowd of morbid onlookers. He remembered the body covered by the sheet. He frowned. "Ferguson's dead?" he said in disbelief. The events of the past two days flashed in his mind, and he asked himself if an entity like Ferguson could actually die. "You've seen the body? You're *sure?*"

"We're pretty sure," the detective started sarcastically. "Those kids beat the shit out of him. His wife is flying in to identify his body. She should be here soon."

At the mention of her, Morton reflexively cringed. He cursed himself in his mind, because the detectives saw his reaction. He looked away from their probing eyes, noticing that the two uniformed officers were still searching his room. One of them was looking under the bed; the other was bent over the garbage can—which was empty, since the maid had changed it earlier. Morton suddenly became aware of his predicament—and the fact that he had not given them permission to search the room. They were looking for evidence to damn him, and he had to stop them before it was too late—

"Hey!" he screamed to the two uniformed officers. "What the hell are you looking for?" And then, addressing the two detectives: "Why are you even here? You just told me you saw the tape. You didn't see me on that tape, did you?"

"You're right, but we're not really here because of that," the one with the lopsided Afro began. "We're here because of this," he said, holding up a manila envelope. When Morton looked, he saw his name was written on it.

"What's that?" he said uneasily. The detective handed it to him. Morton saw it was already open. He lifted the flap and glanced in. He saw a stack of cash, and the wife's picture, and some documents. That was when he remembered: Ferguson had promised to leave him a package! Morton felt faint when he saw how this looked. He walked over to the bed, brushing past the detectives, and sat down heavily. He could sense them staring at him: analyzing his every action. He was trapped! He stared at the floor—

"Why'd he leave you that package, Mr. Morton?" the detective with the bad comb-over started. Morton's mind lurched toward the only escape route he saw:

"He hired me—to spy on his wife."

"Really?" the detective with the lopsided Afro said in a neutral voice. When Morton looked, there was a faint smile on the man's face, as if he knew he had Morton trapped and was only giving Morton time to see the extent of it.

Morton rushed ahead quickly, groping for an escape. "He hired me to keep an eye on her," he said again, "—to *watch* her."

"That's a lot of money for 'watching,'" the detective with the bad comb-over chimed in.

"I'm a good watcher," Morton tried to joke, but it came out flat.

The detective with the lopsided Afro seemed to want to provoke him further: "Why don't you empty out the package: see what exactly he left you?"

Morton nodded his head, as if the detective had given him an order. He emptied the contents of the package by turning it over. There was the cash, several pictures of the wife, and some documents, which, upon precursory glance, seemed like the wife's schedule.

"Why did Ferguson want you to spy on his wife?" asked the detective with the lopsided Afro.

Morton looked up at him cautiously, but the lie/half-truth came easily. "He never said, but it was probably the usual reasons: she's a young, beautiful woman and he's an old man with lots of money."

"He thought she was cheating on him?"

Morton nodded: "He said he *knew* she had a lover."

"How did he know?" This was the one with the bad comb-over.

"I don't think he had anything definite. I guess he was jealous— paranoid. People hire me because they have suspicions they want to prove. That's how it goes. If they had proof, they wouldn't need me."

There was a pause. The detectives stared at him; he stared back, feeling somewhat proud of himself, because he knew he had given them a good answer.

"Have you ever met his wife?" asked the detective with the lopsided Afro.

Morton took a deep breath, in order to give himself time to think through his lie. In those few seconds, he tried to weigh his options. He could say no, but there was the risk of them catching him in a lie. The best course was always to admit to a half-truth: a lie that had pieces of the truth, so that he could continue to lie if the whole truth ever came out. After he released the breath, he said, "I've been trailing her for a few weeks now."

"Is that so?" the one with the lopsided Afro said in the same neutral way. "Was she cheating?"

This time, Morton saw no convenient half-truths. He would have to lie. "Not that I was able to see," he responded.

"Then why was Ferguson paying you so much money?"

"Like I said, he had his suspicions," Morton replied, taking pains to remain calm.

"What was he suspicious *about?*" This was the one with the bad comb-over.

Morton's mind worked frantically again. This time, he used the truth. "She was always going out to dance clubs. She went alone; and of course, she danced with men when she got there. ...And you know how these young girls dance nowadays," he said with an insinuating stare. "Some of those dances are pretty much just fucking with your clothes on."

The detectives smiled. "Did it ever go beyond that?"

"Sometimes she gave out her number to the guys; they were always buying her drinks, and that sort of thing, and she seemed to like it."

"Did the guys ever hook up with her after the club?"

Morton sensed the detective trying to bait him. He had to resist incriminating her. If she had not actually hired those thugs to kill Ferguson, then she and Morton had to protect one another. It occurred to him they would be questioning her soon. They would ask her about him. More likely than not, they would mention Ferguson was having her trailed. Self-preservation told him to incriminate her—to point the arrow of suspicion toward her—but the voice of self-preservation was usually a stupid voice. The world's prisons were full of fools who had "ratted one another out" in an effort to save themselves. Prisons would be much emptier places if all the snitches and co-conspirators had kept their mouths shut.

Morton shook his head: "I never saw her meeting with any of those guys outside the clubs." Then, making another attempt to joke: "You know how these young women are: they like attention more than they like fuckin'. They go into clubs to show themselves off. They do their little dances to get your dick hard, and give you a phone number when you ask for it; but when you call it, it's the Department of Motor Vehicles' hotline number."

The detectives and officers chuckled. The officers had stopped their search and were standing to the rear, listening to him. Morton was relieved. He smiled for the first time. When he glanced down, he saw the money lying on the bed.

"Can I keep this?" he asked, "—or is it evidence?"

"Do you mind if we hold on to it for a day or so?" It was the one with the bad comb-over. He said it as though he were actually asking for permission: as if he were giving Morton a choice. Morton shrugged his shoulders.

The detective with the lopsided Afro came over and started picking up the contents of the package. He added, nonchalantly, "Would you mind coming down to the station for a while?"

"Why?"

He grinned. "Do you really trust us with all this money? Plus, you'd really be doing us a favor if you could make a formal record of everything you just told us."

Morton knew they wanted to interrogate him again—to see if his story changed. He nodded his head, bracing himself for what was to come. This was only a game of cat and mouse. He had done interrogations before—and been interrogated—while he was in the Military. He knew what to expect. They would try to wear him down. He knew the detectives could sense he was not telling the whole truth. He also knew the only way for a mouse to escape a game of cat and mouse was if the cat went chasing after something else. The voice of self-preservation again told him to incriminate the wife, but there was something else to distract the cat, and Morton nodded his head when he realized it.

By now, the detective with the lopsided Afro had returned the items on the bed to the manila envelope—

"I was with him last night," Morton began.

The detectives looked at him confusedly.

"I was with Ferguson yesterday," Morton repeated, "and he was attacked then, too. I managed to scare them off."

"You're just telling us this now?" said the one with the bad comb-over.

"You woke me out of my bed," Morton explained. "I'm still trying to digest that he's dead."

"Did you see the attackers' faces?"

Morton remembered the demonic face when the thug turned to the light; he willed himself not to shudder. "Not clearly, but it must have been the same guys. You should have hotel security check the tapes from last night."

"You didn't report it last night?" asked the one with the lop-sided Afro.

"I wanted to, but Ferguson stopped me. He took me to a bar, instead, to thank me."

"What time did all this take place?" It was the detective with the bad comb-over. He had taken a notepad and pen out of his suit pocket, and had them at the ready.

"About seven, in the same parking lot."

The detectives glanced at one another. "Okay, we'll check it out." It was the one with the bad comb-over. Morton nodded his head: he had sent them on a hunt that would keep them occupied for a while. He was beginning to relax somewhat, but that was when the detective with the bad comb-over added, "Are you ready to come with us?"

Morton looked at them as if lost. "You mean *now*?"

"Sure. May as well get it over with, while the thoughts are still fresh in your mind."

Morton doubted anything was fresh in his mind, and this disturbed him. Yet, there was nothing to do but go with the detectives. He stood up then, and went to his shoes. They were still in the middle of the room, where he had kicked them off.

⁝ ♥ ⁞

Morton rode in the back of the detectives' unmarked sedan. In the front of the car, the two men were in good spirits, and entertained one another by discussing "stupid shit" they had seen lately. Morton's mind was elsewhere. He needed to think: to get his story right, but his mind was going a million miles a minute. He was getting slightly carsick. Outside the car, downtown Orlando passed in a blur. The sight made him feel sicker, so he lay back and closed his eyes.

Presently, the detectives were discussing a young Hollywood actress who had done a sex tape. Of course, by now, it was all over the Internet. The detective with the lopsided Afro said the actress sucked dick with a demented look on her face—as if she were a rabbit chewing a carrot. The two detectives laughed for at least a minute after that one. Morton looked over at them, annoyed. He understood the joke intellectually, but in his current state he could not conjure the good humor required to laugh—

A scratchy voice came over the police radio, and the detectives quieted down. Morton could barely understand any of it, but he thought he heard "shots fired" and "request back-up." Apparently, a location had been given, because the detective with the bad comb-over grabbed the transmitter and told the dispatcher they were in the area, and would arrive within a minute.

They put on the siren and sped up. Morton's queasy feeling intensified. The detective with the lopsided Afro was driving. The man negotiated the corners like a maniac, so that Morton was thrown about like a rag doll. He had his seatbelt on, but it made no difference. They were entering a warehouse district now. The streets were wide and deserted: they did not even have sidewalks. The huge industrial buildings were foreboding in the darkness. Morton looked ahead and saw the flashing lights of the police cruiser. As soon as the vehicle stopped, the two detectives came out with their guns drawn. A uniformed police officer was sitting on the ground, leaning against his cruiser. The detectives went to him—to see if he was shot.

Morton got out of the vehicle. The uniformed officer had stopped an SUV. The occupants of the SUV were splayed on the road. Morton assumed they were dead. He walked over to where the detectives were talking to the uniformed officer. The officer was unresponsive, staring ahead in a daze. The detectives kept asking him what had happened. They shook him; but even then, he only stared ahead, his jaw slack. The detective with the lopsided Afro told his partner to secure the SUV, while he checked the unresponsive officer for injuries. The detective with the bad comb-over ran over to the SUV with his gun drawn. First, he looked in the vehicle, to make sure nobody else was still in there, then he checked the four men on the ground.

"We've got four corpses here," he announced to his partner. In the meantime, the detective with the lopsided Afro had found no wounds. He nodded to his partner. Seeing no immediate danger, the detective with the bad comb-over decided to do a quick sweep of the vehicle. He opened the door and spotted something on the floor. It was a wallet, and when he picked it up and opened it, he yelled, "Holy shit!"

"What is it?" his partner called.

The detective with the bad comb-over walked back over to the police cruiser and handed the wallet to his partner. When he opened it, he looked up at his partner with a stunned look on his face. "It's Ferguson's wallet!" And then, looking at the corpses on the ground, "Those must be the ones who attacked him."

The detective with the bad comb-over pointed to the officer: "What's up with him?"

"Looks like shock. I didn't see any wounds. Whatever happened here, it freaked him out."

"I'll snap him out of it," the detective with the bad comb-over said, stepping up. He began shaking the officer, and telling him to wake up (as if he were only sleeping). Eventually, when the detective seemed on the verge of banging the officer's head against the car, the man seemed to come to his senses. The first thing he did was scream out, and flinch—as if to protect himself from muggers.

"Relax—we're cops!" said the detective with the bad comb-over. At this, the officer seemed to calm down somewhat, but he still seemed to be in shock. When he made an attempt to stand, the detectives helped him up. The man was trembling. He noticed his gun was in his hand. He saw the clip was empty, and went to reload. The detectives gently stopped him. Instead, they encouraged him to tell them what had happened.

For the first time, the man looked toward the SUV—and the figures lying on the asphalt. He jumped. Morton could tell he was still afraid, because he checked his gun again, and reached for his refill clip.

"You're cool now," the detective with the lopsided Afro tried to reassure him. "Just tell us what happened. Are you hurt?"

"I don't think so," the officer said.

"What happened?"

The officer looked back toward the SUV. His face was ashen and sweaty. In the distance, more sirens could be heard.

"Tell us what happened," one of the detectives asked again.

"God," the officer whispered as the images came back to him. "...At first, they were just sitting in the car when I passed. I thought it looked suspicious, so I made a U-turn and came back."

"What happened then?"

"I put on my siren and got out of the car...I took out my gun. When I got there, they were all sitting in there, staring ahead blankly...like they were statues or something. At first, I figured they were high on something. I told them to get out of the car, and keep their hands where I could see them...all the standard stuff...but they just sat there, staring ahead. I banged on the door—to get their attention. That's when the driver turned to me. His face..." The officer faltered.

"What about his face?"

"...I don't know. It was fucked up."

"Fucked up how?" one of the detectives encouraged him.

"It was just...*fucked up*." He could not get over that phrase, and it frustrated him. "...They started to get out of the vehicle— all of them. When I looked, they all had those faces....I shot them. I shot them *all*."

"Don't worry," the detective with the bad comb-over tried to reassure him, "it was obviously self-defense. Plus, these scum-bags were caught on tape murdering a man a few hours ago. You're a hero," he said at last. The officer thought about it. He wanted to believe, but Morton could tell, by his eyes, that he was rethinking everything. He had peeped behind the curtain of the universe and seen an unexpected horror. The officer was where Morton had been two days ago. Morton could practically read the man's mind. His thoughts were poisoning his soul: he would never be the same again. Morton looked away. At that moment, some more police cruisers entered the street. Knowing the scene was going to become more chaotic within a few seconds, Morton headed back to the detectives' sedan.

₭♥ℛ

The detectives stood about the crime scene for another half an hour, while Morton sat in the back of the sedan, trying to clear his head. He closed his eyes, and tried to drown out the sirens and raised voices from all the investigators. He tried to use this time to get his "story" straight in his mind, but it was pointless.

The detectives came back to the car talking excitedly. In addition to the old man's wallet, they had found his Rolex watch in the SUV. The dead thugs had all done time in prison for assault and armed robbery. Eyewitness accounts put them at five other armed robberies this week alone. There were warrants for their arrest. The detectives talked about the case as they sped back to police headquarters. The only thing that bothered them was that the thugs had attacked Ferguson on two consecutive nights. Either the old man had really bad luck, or the thugs had gone out of their way to attack him. Besides that, everything else fit; and from the way the detectives talked openly in front of him, Morton could tell he was no longer a suspect. All he had to do now was repeat everything he had told them, and not give them any reason to look deeper. From his experiences, police officers were inherently lazy: as long as he did not give them any reason to do extra work, he would be fine.

₭♥ℛ

Police headquarters was in a sprawling complex that included a few other municipal offices, like the coroner's office and the morgue. They had to pass through security to get into the building. The detectives, of course, had no problem entering. As Morton was not under arrest, he had to show an ID to get in. Two heavyset, middle-aged, black female officers were running the security station. The detectives flirted with them in a manner that was more habitual than lustful: everyone seemed to expect it, so they carried out their duties. When prompted, Morton dug into his wallet and retrieved his driver's license. The first black woman took it and went to type the information into a database, but then she frowned when she got to his date of birth and looked up at him, saying:

"This says you were born in 1972."

Everyone looked over at Morton. He shrugged: "And?"

"That would make you thirty-five."

"So?" he said, still not catching on.

The woman looked down at his picture again: "You ain't the person on this license." She handed the license over to the other black woman, who looked from the ID picture to Morton, and back again. The other officer tilted her head and scrunched up her face, as if that would allow her to see Morton better:

"He sorta looks like this picture—only he's younger."

Morton remembered the way he looked now; the entire sequence of events flashed in his mind again. The lie came to him quickly: "It's a driver's license," he said as nonchalantly as he could, "the picture always makes you look bad."

The women considered this explanation. The first officer began, "You still don't look thirty-five."

The other one added, "You look like you just graduated high school."

"It must be this healthy Florida air."

They all stared at him, including the detectives. At last, the first female officer looked at the other and shrugged, saying, "It can't be the air: it ain't done nothing for me."

The others all smiled; the detectives began to flirt again, by saying she did not look a day over twenty-two—which was of course a lie.

The female officers finished entering Morton's information into the database. The detectives were asking about taking them out on dates, and the women were declining, but it was an act on all sides: if the women would have said yes, the men would have been stunned; if the detectives had not asked them out, the women would have felt insulted. The act kept everyone happy.

Once the security routine was complete, Morton and the others were buzzed through a door. They entered a wide corridor whose walls were lined with white tiles. With the fluorescent lights blazing overhead, the glare was overpowering. Morton squinted until his eyes adjusted. A handful of officers were walking up and down the corridor. Morton was wondering how long this was going to take when a door at the end of the corridor opened and three people exited. One was Ferguson's wife. The other two were detectives. The wife had to be supported. She was pale and crying. Morton hesitated for a moment, but knew he had to keep walking—lest any of the detectives began to suspect something. The wife and her detectives headed toward Morton, but the wife's head was bowed; she took two steps before her legs gave way. Her detectives managed to grab her. Now, each of them held one of her upper arms and helped her walk down the corridor. In this state, she did not even look up at Morton when he passed, and he was happy for it. However, he stopped and looked back at her—as did his detectives. He noticed the door she had exited from. On top of it were the words "Coroner's Office." She must have just come from identifying Ferguson's body. Yet, as always, Morton wondered if Ferguson could actually be dead: if it was even possible. A side of him knew it was not, and this set off a surge of panic in him. Even when he allowed himself to believe the old man might actually be dead, he remembered that thug from the parking lot—the warped, demonic face. He considered the possibility that hell had sent its minions to collect Ferguson. As the old man had passed on some of his power to Morton, that meant he was also a target for hell's foot soldiers—

"She's definitely a beautiful woman." This was the detective with the lopsided Afro. They were all still standing in the corridor, looking back at her as she was helped down the hall. Morton and the other detective nodded solemnly at the comment, then they turned and continued walking down the corridor. They took Morton to an interrogation room. A video camera was already set up. The detective with the bad comb-over turned it on, then he sat down at the desk. His partner and he were on one side, and Morton was on the other. The camera was set up perpendicular to Morton and the detectives. They prompted Morton, and he began recounting everything he had told them before.

ಬ ♥ ಞ

After about half an hour, the detectives seemed satisfied. The camera was turned off and they were getting ready to leave. Morton's mind kept returning to Ferguson. Through the entire interrogation, his mind had kept asking one question: Could Ferguson really be dead?

As they were heading to the door, he asked, "Can I see the body?"

They looked at him in surprise.

"Ferguson: I want to see him."

The detectives glanced at one another. "Why?" asked the one with the lopsided Afro.

Morton thought about it carefully, but could see no harm in the truth at this point. "I have to know if he's really dead. …Just a few seconds: that's all I'm asking. Nobody'll ever know."

"Why do you care so much about this?" This was the detective with the bad comb-over.

"A man like Ferguson, with all his power and wealth…you wonder if a man like that can really die." Then, as they looked at him oddly, "I know it's a weird request, but I just have to know— so I can move on."

The detective with the lopsided Afro shook his head. "It's not the kind of thing—"

"Please," Morton begged now. "Just a few seconds. Nobody'll ever know."

The detectives looked over at one another. Eventually, they shrugged.

"Okay, come on," began the one with the bad comb-over.

They walked quickly now. Luckily, the corridor was bare. The door was opened with an electronic card. The detective with the bad comb-over swiped his card and then opened the door. The place had an unsavory scent: a combination of vinegar and rancid meat. Morton tried holding his breath. There was an attendant behind a front desk—a man in his early twenties who was eating a meatball sandwich. The sight of the dripping tomato sauce made Morton feel queasy. The detectives were talking to the kid—asking him to let them in without official paperwork. He was bored and indifferent, so he waved them through. The detectives took Morton to the back. A body was still laid out on a central table. It was Ferguson. The sight was sickening: the old man's skull had been shattered; one of his eyes had been ruptured, while the other was bulging out of its socket. On top of that, his teeth had been smashed, so that there were only jagged spikes where his teeth used to be. Morton realized why the wife had been pale. He, too, felt faint and sick. He turned from the sight and began to walk out. He realized he was fleeing: that he was practically jogging. The detectives laughed at him, but he had to get away.

⃞♥⃟

It was about one in the morning when the detectives dropped him off in front of the hotel. They were still laughing at him. He could not really care at this point. He knew he was a mess. When he got up to his room, he still felt unreal. He looked about the room as if lost. His eyes went to the windows. The blinds were open. Instinctively, he went to them, and shut them. It was not until he was finished that he remembered what Ferguson had said about always keeping the blinds closed. Not only was Ferguson his father: he was beginning to act like the man. The realization brought an unsettled feeling over him, so that he meandered over to the bed and sat down heavily. He grasped his head in his hands. He was losing it. To distract his thoughts, he decided to turn on the television. Ferguson's murder was the headline story on the news. The caption on the TV read, "Famous Financier Murdered in Street Crime." There were images of Ferguson mingling at fundraisers and other staged publicity events. All of it was fake; more troublingly, even though Morton had seen the man's corpse with his own eyes, he knew it was not over.

Morton noticed that reports on the prostitute were gone now. Today, she was literally yesterday's news. He turned off the television after about five minutes, swearing he would leave this place in the morning—no matter what.

ℝ♥℞

The telephone rang. He was aware of it ringing, but it was as if he were hearing it from far off in the distance. It chimed four times before he escaped from sleep and opened his eyes. He looked at the phone. As it was chiming a sixth time, he picked it up.

"Yes?" he answered, drowsily.

"Mr. Morton?" asked a woman.

"Yes."

"I'm calling from the police department. We're calling to say you can pick up your package."

Morton had to think for a few seconds before he realized what she was talking about. "Okay, thanks." And then, as something occurred to him, "I guess you won't need it for the investigation?"

"I guess not." As she said it, Morton realized she was probably only a low-level secretary, and had no idea what was going on with the investigation. But then she added, "Mrs. Ferguson said it was okay."

"Mrs. Ferguson?" he whispered.

"Yes, sir, she was just in here, clearing up some loose ends. The investigation is pretty much over."

Just in there? Morton thought to himself. That was when he looked over at his alarm clock and saw it was three-fifteen in the afternoon! "What the hell...?" he whispered into the phone receiver.

"What?" the woman on the phone said.

"I'm sorry," Morton said, still in shock. "I didn't realize it was this late. I have to go. Thanks for calling." He hung up the phone. He sat up in bed and looked around. The blinds were still closed. He could see daylight creeping into the room at the corners; but otherwise, the room was cast in darkness. He got out of bed and went over to the windows. When he opened the blinds, he saw it really was the middle of the afternoon. He frowned. It did not seem possible. He wondered why the maid had not awakened him when she came to clean the room. Deciding to check something, he went to the entrance and opened the door. The "Do Not Disturb" sign was on the outer doorknob. He frowned again: he could not remember putting it on the door.

Eventually, he shook his head and closed the door. He had wanted to be back home by now. He had wanted to put this place behind him, and forget all the nightmare events. A side of him was beginning to believe he would never leave. Something was conspiring to keep him here. He shook his head, knowing such thoughts would only push him further over the edge.

He decided to check out of the hotel now. The next plane to Atlanta left around nine at night. In the interim, he could check out, pick up his money and return his rental car. The important thing is to get out of here and put distance between himself and the horrors of the last few days.

In fifteen minutes, he was ready to go. He had never been a heavy traveler anyway. He looked around the room one last time, to make sure he had not left anything. When he was satisfied, he left quickly. However, when the elevator opened and he stepped into the lobby, he saw the wife enter the building. A bellhop had to help her along; after a few steps, he waved for assistance, and a manager ran up to help. The wife seemed semi-conscious at best—as if her soul had been drained. Morton felt sorry for her. Oftentimes, people wished harm on others without fully realizing what they were wishing for. After all her schemes to kill the old man, she had finally seen what she had been hoping for. The sickening sight of the old man's corpse would be with her forever. Morton had been to war and even he had been sickened by the sight of the old man's corpse. The wife now had everything she had ever wanted. She was free of Ferguson and had the old man's immense wealth, but Morton doubted she would ever be happy again. She would have to go back to the old man's mansion by herself, and everything in that godforsaken place would remind her of Ferguson.

The hotel was getting a wheelchair for the wife. Her entire body now drooped, as if her bones were slowly melting within her. Morton turned his back on it all, and went to check out.

₨♥ℓ

Morton picked up Ferguson's package from the police department and returned to Atlanta. Once he got back to his apartment, the first thing he did was close all the curtains and blinds. He only had a studio apartment, but he searched the place, as if some monster were hiding in the smallest crevice, waiting for him to go to sleep before it sprang out. He searched for half an hour—even though he could see the entire place by turning his head from side to side. After searching, he watched some television, then he searched again. He could not free himself of the fear that he had missed something, so he kept rechecking the same spots and corners, like a madman. It was not until about three in the morning that he finally allowed himself to close his eyes; but even then, it was more a matter of exhaustion than a choice to go to sleep. Worse, the moment he lost consciousness, he saw the same terrible images he had seen after the shadow bird attacked him. However, instead of hundreds of flashing images, a single scene played in his mind. He was in an immense field. It was just after sunset, but something was lighting up the sky. He felt the heat source on his skin, and smelled smoke; and when he turned to the right, he saw that a huge mansion was burning. The mansion was only two stories high, but the flames seemed to reach up to the sky—

Something exploded then, and he squinted and ducked down. However, when he looked up again, he noticed there were black people dancing and chanting around a plant. They were not too far from him, and as he looked more closely, he saw the plant was the same rose bush he had seen the last time. It had huge white blossoms; and as before, it emanated a dark power that made his skin crawl. The people dancing and chanting about the rose bush seemed to be slaves, by the looks of their tattered clothes; the burning mansion seemed to be the slave mansion... but whatever was going on, the rose bush was demonic—the source of dark, unimaginable power. His soul rebelled against it, and the entire scene. It was a brutal fight; but at last, he regained consciousness and opened his eyes.

The dream or recollection or whatever it was, disappeared. He should have been relieved; but he realized, in those first moments of groggy consciousness, that something in the apartment had awakened him. There had been a muffled sound in the silence—something like a footstep or a man clearing his throat. Now that he sniffed the air, there was an unsavory scent—like something long dead that had recently been unburied. Morton jumped up, his eyes darting about his apartment. With the closed blinds on the windows, there was a kind of twilight darkness about the place. He glanced at his alarm clock, seeing that it was after two in the afternoon. Like everything else, time seemed disconnected and unreal. He sat up in the bed like a scared child, listening for any telling noise: any sign that there might actually be someone in the apartment with him. He sniffed the air again, trying to decide if the scent of newly uncovered death was only a figment of his imagination. As the panic grew in him, he turned on the light on the nightstand, so he could get a better view of the apartment. Maybe two more minutes passed before he felt it was safe to get out of bed. He went to the window first, and opened the blinds, to let in the light, and then he checked the apartment again, searching every corner and crevice. In fact, he was a nervous wreck for the entire day, jumping at every unexpected sound....

The second day, it was the same thing. He awoke from the same dream—the same nightmare of the demonic rose bush—but by now, he realized it was not just a nightmare. It was something that had actually happened: an event from the distant past that had been branded on his soul for all eternity. As he opened his eyes and returned to the world of the present, there were the same phantom sounds and scents about the apartment. Like the first day, after the initial panic passed, he began to check the apartment again. However, knowing he was on a slippery slope to madness, he stopped himself and got out of the house. It was already about three in the afternoon. He dressed haphazardly, throwing on whatever was about. On the staircase, he saw one of his neighbors: an elderly lady who squinted at him, then gasped when she saw how young he looked. He rushed away quickly—before her questions rekindled the panic within him.

He walked the neighborhood for an hour or so, staring ahead blankly like a sleepwalker. It was by accident that he came upon the library. As a private detective, he had used the library's microfilm facilities to do background checks on people he was investigating. He had done a precursory check on Ferguson a month ago, but something told him to check again—to see if he had missed anything. The last twenty years of newspaper articles were standard: philanthropic donations and society events and corporate triumphs. Everything Ferguson had ever touched had turned to gold. Morton had been about to turn away and return home when it occurred to him he had not gone far enough back into Ferguson's past. He was looking up an article on Ferguson's birth when he realized all the listings for Templeton Ferguson IV began a week after Templeton Ferguson III had died. The first article was from 1926—when he supposedly returned from Europe to see to his father's affairs. In the article, there was a picture of a dapper-looking young man. Morton leaned in closer: the man in the picture was literally a white version of him! Morton sat staring at the picture for a minute or two, his mind working frantically. Instinct told him to check the death of Templeton Ferguson II. The librarian had to retrieve the articles from the historical archives in the bowels of the library. The documents were from 1852. Morton felt a chill go through him when he saw the records. Once again, the heretofore unmentioned heir (Templeton Ferguson II) returned from Europe after his father's death. The pictures in the collection showed the region's planter class and their holdings. In many of the pictures, masters posed with their slaves. Babies appeared with their wet nurses; young boys appeared beside the stable boys of their ponies. When Morton searched the documents, he saw a picture of the same dapper-looking young man as before! In the picture, young Ferguson was sitting regally on a leather chair, with his house slaves standing at his back: the courtiers of his palace. Young Ferguson's pose was erect; his face was smug with the comforts that came with wealth and power. Morton's mouth gaped: there could be no doubt that it was the same man from 1926. Somehow, Ferguson was immortal!

The archives had no listing for Templeton Ferguson I, but in his heart, Morton knew it was all the same man. Ferguson had to be at least one hundred and seventy years old! Morton's mouth gaped, and when his eyes rested on one of the servants standing behind young Ferguson, he gasped. He leaned closer to make sure, but there was no doubt: the servant was the old woman from the swamp. Not only that: in the picture, she was the same age as when he saw her a few days ago. She, too, had to be immortal....

Morton fled from the library, unable to see or to think or to feel. He returned home, and tried to make sense of it all, but it was impossible. He turned on the television to distract himself, but there was a report that Ferguson's funeral was going to be tomorrow. World leaders and other men of wealth and power were expected to attend. Morton only stared ahead blankly. Eventually, he managed to sleep, but when he closed his eyes, he saw the same nightmare images of slaves dancing around the rose bush; and when he opened his eyes in the morning, there was the same sense that someone else was in the apartment with him. There was the same unsavory scent in the air. He checked the apartment; but by now, it was more out of routine than because he actually expected to find anything. He sighed, then recalled that today was Ferguson's funeral.

He looked over at the alarm clock on his nightstand. It was a quarter to two in the afternoon. By now, Ferguson had already been eulogized. At that moment, the coffin was probably on the way to the cemetery. Morton figured there was still time to get to the cemetery for the burial and final rites. Maybe seeing the old man's casket being lowered into the ground would free him from the delusion that the old man was about to come back to life. He lay in bed for a few minutes, considering the pros and cons of going. …He needed closure. He had spent the preceding days struggling to get back to what he had, but he knew now he had been going about it the wrong way. He had been struggling to get back to something that did not exist any-more—and which would never exist again. That side of him was dead and gone. Ahead of him, there was a struggle—a journey into the next phase of his life. It was not a journey that could be quantified by time or distance or any other tangible meas-urement. Instead, it was something spiritual—a threshold of faith and understanding that he had to surpass. He could not explain it, but he sensed that seeing Ferguson being lowered into his grave might be the first step in that long journey. He nodded his head and began to get ready.

He already knew which cemetery Ferguson had been taken to. He had collected the information the day before—during his restless moments. His black suit was already ironed and hanging in his closet. In the bathroom, the sight of his youthful face had become less of a shock. He barely needed to shave anymore.

When he got out of the bathroom, he noticed Ferguson's package of money was still on his dresser. He had counted out the bills during another of his restless moments. Including the unspent money from his dealings with the wife, he now had $15,000 in cash. He knew he should take it to the bank, or invest it, or do something productive with it, but his obsession with Ferguson kept him from acting.

Ten minutes later, he was in the car, headed to the cemetery. He became aware he was not hungry. He had barely eaten yesterday either—as if he were being fed by an unknown, unseen power. He looked at his reflection in the rearview mirror. His youthful, handsome face mocked him—especially as he knew it was Ferguson's face. …Ferguson was his father. The thought still made his stomach clench. A new fit of restlessness came over him, so that he could barely sit still in the car seat. *Calm down*, he told himself, but it was useless, and he *knew* it was useless, because he had been telling himself the same thing for the last five days.

As he neared the cemetery, he got in a traffic jam and realized he was behind the funeral procession. There were so many cars that he had to park outside the cemetery and walk in. There were news vans in the parking lot: all the major networks. This was the final act in the entire sordid play, and none of the stations wanted to miss it.

He followed the stream of black-clothed people. There had

to be at least five thousand people. Maybe there were as many as ten or fifteen thousand people. Morton shuffled along, shoulder-to-shoulder with them. The wife: thoughts of her suddenly became a motivating force to him. It was not love or a sexual longing or anything like that, but instead the need to commiserate with someone who might understand what he felt inside. He remembered the image of her coming out of the coroner's office. Her mind, soul and body had been brutalized. All about her, there had been the same mortal terror that he now felt inside. In the entire world, she was probably the only person who might understand what he had been through.

In the distance, perhaps two hundred meters away, he made out what he assumed to be the gravesite. An impassable crowd of thousands had gathered around it. Morton sighed, knowing he would not even get to see the wife. She was no doubt in the center of the crowd, crying on the side of the gravesite as the preacher said final rites. His pace slowed; stragglers in the funeral procession brushed past him. Morton was considering turning back when some people to his right chorused, "Amen!"

When Morton looked in that direction, his insides went cold. In the middle of about fifty black people, was the old woman from the swamp—and the plantation picture. She was giving her own eulogy. Morton found himself going in that direction. Soon, he was in the midst of them. They noticed him there; the old woman smiled when she saw him; the others made space for him. He moved ahead slowly—as if in a trance. Eventually, he noticed the black people were all young boys. They were arrayed in an assortment of patched suits and hand-me-downs. The oldest one was perhaps seventeen. Morton's eyes widened: all the boys looked like him—were little black versions of Ferguson.

They were still making space for Morton within their gathering. Indeed, in a matter of seconds, he was standing in the middle with the old woman. Looking to the left, Morton saw the two little boys from the swamp were there as well. He remembered that they were his brothers—and that the old woman was impossibly old. As he was thinking these thoughts, she grasped him by the shoulders. He looked down at her joyous face as she said, "Something great's gonna happen! You all feel it, don't you?" Here, she looked past Morton, to the rest of Ferguson's bastard sons—

"This is what we've been waiting for!" the old woman rejoiced now. All around her, Ferguson's bastard sons nodded their heads or groaned in agreement. "People think he's dead," the old woman continued, "—but we know better!" She let go of Morton's shoulder now, and began pacing the outer edge of the crowd, staring into the eyes of her de facto congregation. "Yes, they think he's dead, but he'll be rising up soon, claiming his place at the right hand of God!"

The others began to exult. Affirmative "Amens" and "Preach, mother!" were shouted. Morton saw it all then. They were not merely Ferguson's bastards: they were his cult. More than that, they saw Morton as a natural member—maybe even an exalted member, since Ferguson had endowed him with his power.

Morton began to back away. He pushed past them. They called to him, and tried to hold him back, and keep him in the fold, but he fled. Once he was free of them, he ran. He felt light-headed and short of breath, but he willed himself to keep going. Once he was in the car, he took off at full speed. His hands were trembling on the steering wheel. He was sweating, and there was a sick taste in his mouth, as if his insides were rotting.

As it was Atlanta, he was soon stuck in a traffic jam. He sat fidgeting in his seat. He asked himself where he was going. He knew he did not want to go home. He did not exactly want to be alone; at the same time, he knew there was no one he could talk to. The traffic jam was inching toward the off ramp. He decided to go to the mall: he would be able to be around other people, and it would be a way to waste some time.

In the mall, he walked around aimlessly for about half an hour. He passed the same shops and the same people. At one point, some fourteen-year-old girls giggled coquettishly as he passed. Initially, he looked at them confusedly, but then he remembered how young and handsome he looked now. He stopped and stared at his reflection in one of the store's display windows. His suit gave him a sophisticated yet rakish look. He should have been pleased, but he remembered he was watching Ferguson's face. He shook his head and walked on.

He decided to see a movie—to waste more time. He saw an action flick. The plot was predictable, and this annoyed him—especially as he was barely paying attention. After the movie, he considered other places he might go to waste time, but he was not in the mood for clubs or bars, so he headed home. Mercifully, the traffic had thinned by then.

ဆာ ♥ ∞

In the morning, he awoke the same way he had awakened on the previous mornings. Nightmare images of the rose bush and demonic slave ritual had tortured him in his sleep. When he opened his eyes, he heard a noise—dull footfalls across his floor—and sprang up in bed. The sickening smell of newly uncovered death was there. All the other mornings, he had stared into the empty space of his apartment; but this time, when he looked, Ferguson was there! The old man was at the foot of his bed, grinning down at him. Before Morton had time to scream, the image faded. The grinning face became transparent, and then it was gone, and Morton was left sitting there hyperventilating—

The phone on his nightstand rang. He practically leapt out of bed to get away from it. When he saw it was only the phone, he disentangled himself from the sheet and answered it, but he was still panting and anxious.

"Yes?"

"It's me—I need you!" It was the wife. Even after he recognized her voice, Morton could only stare into space; and then, remembering the old man had been at the foot of his bed, he stared in that direction. He wanted to believe it had only been a dream—the vestiges of a nightmare fading back into the nothingness—but he felt doomed. "—Are you there?" asked the wife again.

"Yeah," he said, coming to his senses. He glanced at his alarm clock. It was two-forty in the afternoon. "What's wrong?" he asked.

"Can you come over?"

He frowned: "To your place?" They had never met at Ferguson's mansion before. The huge plantation was about forty minutes outside of the city. There had been pictures of it in the archives, of course, but actually going there seemed like tempting fate—

"Please, baby," the wife begged, "—I'm losing it." She began to cry.

"What's going on?" he started cautiously.

"I need you."

There was a pause. He looked at his clock warily—not that he had anywhere else to go or be. "Now?" he hedged.

"Yes, now. Please. I'm *losing* it," she said again, between sobs.

Morton remembered his thoughts at the funeral: the wife might be the only other person in the world who understood what he was going through. He had known he was losing it for about five days now. Maybe the wife would be a crucial anchor back to something he had lost. "...Okay," he said eventually. "I'll be there in an hour."

However, after he put down the phone and was standing there alone, the entire sequence of events played in his mind, and he groaned.

₭♥⁝

He had to use his car's navigation system to get out to Ferguson's mansion. Objectively speaking, the place he saw in those historical pictures had been magnificent. It was one of those white plantation mansions with Roman columns in the front. Yet, while he was watching grainy, black-and-white pictures of it, Morton's mind had gone to the horrors of the slaves, who had built up something they would never be able to enjoy....

The last couple of roads to Ferguson's mansion were narrow and winding. It was nearing four in the afternoon. By now, Morton could barely think. All his panic and restlessness had short-circuited his mind and body, so that he only stared ahead blankly as he followed the disembodied female voice on the car's navigation system.

He stopped in front of the gate. The mansion was up on a

hill, about three hundred meters away. He sat staring at it. Houses in horror movies were always grand and imposing from the outside: places of extraordinary wealth that hid inconceivable nightmares within their walls. With a shudder, Morton realized this was the mansion he had seen burning in his recurring nightmare/vision. Ferguson must have had it rebuilt after the slave insurrection or whatever it had been.

There was an intercom system on his side of the gate. He pressed the button. After about five seconds, an old black man answered. In Morton's mind, he saw an Uncle Ben's caricature: a good, old-time darkie in a tuxedo with tails. Morton shook his head to free himself of the image. "I'm here to see Mrs. Ferguson. I'm Charles Morton—I'm expected."

"Yes, sir," said the old darkie, and the gates began to open, as if by magic.

Morton drove slowly up the driveway. There was a sprawling lawn from the gate to the house. Seven or eight football fields could easily have fit in it. Back in slavery days, this was probably all farmland. In Morton's mind, he saw hundreds of slaves bent over in the heat, picking the master's cotton. He saw their wretched perspiration-drenched faces so vividly that he clamped his eyes shut and took a deep breath.

When he opened his eyes again, he noticed an oddly placed shrub on the left side of the driveway. By now, he was about halfway between the gate and the house. Something about the shrub called to him. It was the only one in the yard, and that drew attention to it. He slowed the car as he neared it. It was about fifty meters to the left. He squinted: it was a rose bush, with huge white flowers. It was *the* rose bush! His stomach clenched; his mind reeled from the possibilities. Indeed, goose bumps formed on his skin as he sat staring at it. He could sense there was something demonic about it: an evil presence—

He forced his mind to move on to something else. He pressed on the accelerator again, to move away from the bush and all the insane thoughts flowing through his head. Unfortunately, he was moving closer to the mansion, and this fact only deepened his sense of doom. The building was ominous. He asked himself why he had even come to this place. He remembered the wife's tears during the phone call, and realized her distress had manipulated him into coming. It was not too late to turn around and flee. He considered it, but where was he to go now? The wife had said she was losing her mind, and Morton could relate. Maybe, he, too, needed someone with whom he could talk and commiserate. Maybe, if they put their heads together, he and the wife could find some kind of defense against the horrors of the last week.

After he parked in front of the building, its grand entrance-way opened, and the old darkie stood there with a straight back and a haughty, disinterested expression on his face. The man looked exactly as Morton had imagined—including the tuxedo—and this disturbed him. With the exception of Morton's car, they could have been back in the 1800s. Morton tried not to think of it as he got out of the car and walked up to the butler.

The interior of the house was magnificent: the product of generations of wealth. The old darkie led Morton through it, then pointed toward Mrs. Ferguson's "parlor." The butler then turned and walked away, as if he faced some kind of reprimand if he walked any farther.

The wife was sitting on a red velvet settee. Her eyes were red from tears. When he entered the door, she leapt up and ran to him. She was in a flowing silk nightgown. She was beautiful.

Morton had to brace himself against that realization. She was hugging him now. Her body felt good next to his. She began to sob again, so he held her tighter.

"It's okay," he said to reassure her. He rubbed her back. "What's this all about?" he asked at last, disengaging from her a little, so he could look at her face.

"Everything's crazy," she began. "I just got a call from the lawyer." She paused and looked up at him in bewilderment: "Ferguson left half his money to his son."

"His son?" Morton whispered, his face creasing.

She nodded. "What did you find when you drove down to that place? Were there kids there?" she asked, looking distraught.

Morton took a deep breath. There was nothing to do but tell her the truth: "Yeah, there were kids. …He has dozens of kids."

"What!"

"Yeah—all black. …They were at his funeral, too."

She frowned. "Did they have his name?"

"What do you mean?"

"He left his money to Templeton Ferguson V."

Morton's eyes widened, but it was the final piece of the puzzle, and he nodded his head. Ferguson was going to come back, just as he had come back before—

"I don't think he's dead," the wife said abruptly.

Morton looked at her.

"I think he's back. I *saw* him," she said, trembling.

Morton stared at her for three or four seconds before he risked saying anything. He began cautiously: "What did you see?"

"…I've had this feeling…since I came back from Florida. I know I identified his body, but even back then, I knew he wasn't dead."

Morton fidgeted; when she saw his reaction, she frowned and looked at him anew.

"You've felt it, too, haven't you?" She stood up straighter, letting go of him so she could observe him better.

He sidestepped her question by asking a question: "You say you saw him?"

She nodded uneasily as the thoughts came back to her. "This morning, when I woke up, he was there. I got a glimpse of him, then he disappeared...God, I screamed. The maid thought I was crazy—wanted to call the hospital."

"What do you think is happening?" he asked, searching for a plausible explanation for his own fears.

She shook her head. "Things ain't right. That's all I know: things ain't right." She remembered something then, and looked up at him anxiously: "He told me this story once, about how his great-grandfather made a deal with the devil to get back his slaves. ...I've been dreaming that I was one of his slaves. I've dreamed it every night since he died."

Morton wanted to tell her everything then: that he was Ferguson's son; that Ferguson was at least one hundred and seventy years old, and that both their souls were in danger, but he could not see the use. The old adage was false: the truth did not set you free: it only complicated matters. The only thing that mattered now was finding a way to escape the fates they had foolishly cast for themselves. "You've got to get away," he said now, "—leave, before it's too late."

"Come with me," she responded quickly, as if she had been thinking the same thing, herself.

"Me?" he said, surprised.

"He's after us. Don't you see that? He's back for us. He knows the things we did. I always knew he did," she said, looking off to the side. "I always pretended he didn't know what was going on, but I always knew I was fooling myself." She paused for a moment, losing herself in her thoughts. When she looked up at him again, she seemed to see him for the first time. She frowned. "You look different—younger."

The question made him anxious. He did not want to go into it, so he shook his head.

She searched his face, still frowning. Her eager eyes made him uneasy, yet there was something about her eyes that made her seem like a real person, instead of a crude archetype of a gold-digging wife. She was beautiful, stripped of all her greed and schemes. For the first time in a month, he felt he was seeing the real her. As for her, she was still surveying his face—trying to make sense of his youthful appearance. Eventually, she sighed. "I guess I never really saw you before," she mused, attributing his youthful appearance to her previous blindness.

Despite everything that had happened, he smiled. "You like what you see?"

She smiled as well, and held him close again. After a few moments, she said, "I've been stupid about so many things." When he looked down at her, she continued, "Come away with me, baby. Let's get far away from here. We can go to the tropics— anywhere you want. I'll pay for everything," she added. She was hugging him tightly now—as if she were begging him with her body. She trembled and seemed fragile in his arms. "Please," she said again, practically squeezing the breath out of him.

"Okay," he said helplessly, giving in to her fears and his.

When he assented, she reached up and kissed him quickly on the neck, then nuzzled her face in his chest. She smelled good. He breathed deeply and took her in. ...And her skin and body had always felt good. He rubbed her upper back as he pulled her to him. He could feel her breasts pressing against him: her silk nightgown was skimpy. He held her tighter, and she could tell, by the stiffening of his body, that he was becoming aroused. As she had always loved the power she had over aroused men, she smiled and gently sucked his neck. The sensation this caused was like an electric shock: his body convulsed. He moved his hand down, to her backside. It was firm and round. He grasped it, and began kneading the supple flesh. Now, he bent his head and began kissing her. She stood on her tiptoes to reach him. Her tongue was warm and velvety in his mouth. His right hand went to her full breast, and squeezed. *Damn*, he thought to himself, she was perfect, and he could see no point in trying to resist her. He did not bother to make sense of it anymore: he only knew he wanted her. Her body was in his arms, and he would take it.

Either he pushed her over to the settee or she pulled him. Maybe it was a combination of the two. In those moments, the outside world ceased to exist; the last few days of terror and uncertainty were forgotten. He pulled her nightgown over her head, and then he lowered her to the settee. She was naked underneath the nightgown, and he paused for a moment and looked at her, surveying every succulent curve. She let him watch her, reveling in the hunger she saw reflected in his eyes. She allowed her knees to part, so he could get an unobstructed view of her sex. She smiled when she saw his lustful stare. He practically flung himself at her—like a wild animal attacking prey. His mouth went to her right breast. His left hand kneaded the other breast. She moaned and he moaned. After a few moments, his mouth moved over to the other breast. He was hungry: he would devour her if he could. In his pants, his erection was so hard and full that its confinement in his underwear was slightly painful. In his hunger, he sucked up half her breast into his mouth; she gasped and arched her back. He wanted to taste all of her. His hunger spread through him like a kind of madness, and he did not resist it. His mouth moved down, to her abdomen and belly button…down to the parting of her legs. He used his tongue to separate her labia. Her juices were thick and hot and tangy. She grabbed the back of his head and pulled him to her. She ground her pelvis into his face. She had not shaved her pubic hair in a few days, and the short, sharp hairs scratched his face. He did not care. Her body was shuddering now. He grasped her hips and held on, as if he feared he would be flung off a roller coaster.

After the first raw wave of pleasure washed over her, she grabbed his hair to stop him, then pulled his head off her. She was panting, her eyes veiled with passion. "Strip," she said, gasping for air. It was either an order or a plea. He rose and complied. There were two ways to strip: slow and seductive, or quickly, as to get to the business at hand. This was the time to get down to business, so he pulled off his jacket and flung it over his shoulder. He was in jeans. In a brusque motion, his pants and his underwear were at his knees. He kicked them, and his shoes, off, then he went to her. She stared at his body, genuinely in awe of it. He was youthful and strong and felt as though he could make love to her for hours. He wanted to do it to her repeatedly—until they were both sore and exhausted.

He propped up her leg on the back of the settee and entered her in one smooth motion. He felt her muscles fighting him every step of the way, but he persevered until he was in her up to the hilt. They both gasped, and paused for an instant—as if they were in shock and had to brace themselves for what was to come. Morton had never felt this way before. It did not merely feel good to be inside of her: he felt on the verge of something incredible. She was still staring up at him as if stunned. His hips began to move. The sensation was incredible: like being touched by God. He felt himself infused with primordial energy. He groaned; spasms went through his body; somewhere, far off, he heard the wife cry out. His vision was blurry. His hips were moving faster; but by now, the pleasure that had been confined to his penis now spread through his entire body; with every stroke, his body took in more of the primordial energy and carried him off to a god-like place. He was seeing spots before his eyes now; the room was a blur; far off in the distance, the wife was still screaming out. He, too, was screaming as the pleasure of the gods seized him. It was like the big bang, or an atomic blast: the release of unimaginable amounts of energy. For a moment, it was as if his entire body were blown to bits— as if the pleasure had popped him, like a balloon filled past its limit. He felt like pieces of his body were thrown everywhere, shredded from the explosion. In the chaotic aftermath, he slid off the wife's body; maybe thirty seconds to a minute passed before he felt like he had a definite body again. He first became aware of the floor beneath him, and the effect of gravity. As he opened his eyes and blinked, he saw the room beginning to take shape again. He stared at the high ceiling, and the crystal chandelier hanging from it. The dwindling sunlight from out-side the window reflected off it, causing geometric sparkles to form before his eyes. He squinted to mitigate the effect. He felt high—as if he had consumed a forbidden drug. Yet, he smiled: he felt amazing. A side of him wanted to doze, but he remembered the wife. He wanted more of her. His erection, he realized sud-denly, was still there, and ready.

He turned his head and looked up at the settee—

The sickening sight made him scurry away! His carefree smile left him, replaced by a scowl. Where the wife's beautiful, supple body used to be, there was now a dried husk: something that looked like a mummified corpse. All at once, Morton remembered what had happened with the prostitute. It was the same thing all over again; and when the full extent of it occurred to him, he put his trembling hand to his mouth. Ferguson had damned him—taken his revenge. Morton got to his feet. He was still dizzy, but he realized he was dizzy from the overload of power he felt inside. He had sucked up the wife's soul—her power. Her strength was a hundred times that of the prostitute's. There was no comparison. He felt the power trying to bust through his skin; for those first few moments, he held himself tensely, as if afraid relaxing would cause the power to blow him to bits again—

He had to get away from this place. He began to move to the door when he looked down and saw he was still naked. His erection was still there, mocking him. He grabbed his pants from off the floor and put them on. He did not bother with his jacket or shoes. None of those things mattered. He only wanted to cover his erection: the source and reminder of his damnation.

He fled from the mansion. He sprinted through it, amazed by the power of his muscles—the ease with which his body moved through the air. Indeed, despite the horror of what had happened, he felt like a god—as though he could do anything. He had tapped into something no mortal man had the right to access. He still had no idea what he would do or where he would go, but he knew he had to get away and think.

When he opened the front door and looked out on the great

lawn before him, he stopped—as if afraid of the darkening world. He felt suddenly vulnerable, as if sensing a predator lurking. His car was still in the driveway. He ran for it. As soon as he was in it, he put it in gear and pressed on the accelerator. As he escaped, he looked up and saw the old darkie standing in the open doorway. The man's face was still implacable and disinterested. He hated the man then, just as he hated the old woman from the swamp, and all the house niggers who had willingly sacrificed their souls to a devil. He had to get away before he became one of them.

He stamped on the accelerator and headed down the long driveway. That was when he looked ahead and saw the bush. *The rose bush...*the nightmare images came back to him; he considered the dark power he had always felt lurking within it, and all those slaves dancing around it, carrying out their heathen rituals. They had all been like Ferguson's bastard sons at the funeral, empowering their collective devil. Before the thought was fully formed in Morton's mind, he steered the car off the driveway, and onto the lawn. Soon, the rose bush was in his sights. He had sensed the thing's power before. Its power was Ferguson's power. He stomped on the accelerator: if he obliterated the plant, he would obliterate the source of Ferguson's power. He was screaming out now, with the hate and brutal will it took to destroy something powerful.

When he hit the bush, it uprooted and banged into his windscreen, shattering it. He swerved the steering wheel, but it was pointless. The bush came through the windscreen, stabbing him in the face. Before he had time to react, the car flipped. He was not wearing his seatbelt, so he was wrenched about like a rag doll in a dog's jaws. By the time the car stopped flipping, he was sure he was dead. In fact, he knew he should have been, but with the power inside of him, any wounds he had sustained were healed in milliseconds. He touched his face: there was not even a scratch.

He got out of the car. He looked at his arms and bare torso. There was not even a bruise. He was immortal. He stared ahead in shock—

There was a laugh behind him. When Morton looked, he saw Ferguson standing there, grinning at him. The old man smelled like death; his clothes and face were covered with dirt, as if he had just dug himself out of his grave. "Thanks for getting rid of that goddamn bush for me," Ferguson began. "That son of a bitch had me trapped for over two hundred years."

Morton took a step back. Even though he still felt the power, he instinctively knew he was outmatched. He retreated another step.

"Ain't no use in running now, boy," Ferguson said as if disappointed. Yet, Morton retreated another step, and tripped over a piece of the butchered rose bush. Ferguson laughed at him. "It was your nigger kin that planted that bush, boy. They thought they would punish me—trap my soul in there, simply because I was carrying out nature's will. You *freed* me, boy," he said, seeming almost grateful. "I knew you was the key to it all— that's why I gave you the power. You sucked up that bitch wife for me," he said with a laugh. "She had everything I needed— all the power I needed to grow strong again—but she just wasn't my taste," he said with a sly smile. "You see," he said, stepping up to Morton with a playful stroll, "my pappy could get his power from women, but I get my power the other way." As he said these last words, he sprang at Morton, laughing, his face horrible.

Morton tried to push him off—to beat him off—but he was

suddenly paralyzed. The old man's hands and tongue were on him. Morton screamed out at the horror of it...but it was too late. Morton felt all his power being sucked up. Everything he had gotten from the wife was leaving him now. A strange sensation came over him, as if he were shrinking. Once again, his vision became blurry; it became harder and harder to think, so that after a while, Morton's mind and soul were literally blank.

Minutes later, when he regained consciousness, he had no idea who he was or where he was. When he looked up, he saw a young, dapper man. It was Ferguson. Morton was still on the ground. He stood up now, and saw he was naked. His jeans were on the ground. Rather, the jeans of a grown man were on the ground: Morton was now a child: a four-year-old, staring up at his smiling father. As he looked up, he saw the old black woman appear at Ferguson's side, with dozens of other black boys—Ferguson's sons. The old woman's eyes were red, burning slits, and Morton stared at her in amazement. She had always been the shadow bird, bringing escaped slaves back to their master. Even though this knowledge was no longer accessible or meaningful to him in his blank, childish state, on a spiritual level, he sensed that something monstrous had just happened to him. He began to cry now, but he cried as a child cried. All the details of the past month were gone. The only thing he knew for sure was that he was sad and confused and utterly vulnerable. He sobbed louder, but Ferguson came up to him then, shushing him gently—almost lovingly. Then, at last, when Morton's cries became somber and hushed, Ferguson sniggered, saying, "Y'all goddamn niggers are so predictable: the more power I give you, the more power you bring back to me."

ABOUT THE AUTHOR

D.V. Bernard is the critically acclaimed author of four novels. For more information on his work, you can visit his website: www.dvbernard.com

HOW TO KILL YOUR
Boyfriend

Dr. Vera Alexander got out of the cab and stood looking at the storefront bookshop. It was in Midtown Manhattan—one of those trendy neighborhoods where everything cost too much and the droves of shoppers took a strange kind of pride from the fact that they were squandering their money. Vera surveyed her reflection in the bookstore's windowpane. She was a slightly plump 31-year-old who always had a tendency to look overdressed. The socially acceptable stereotype at the moment was that gay men had impeccable fashion sense, so she trusted all her clothing, hair and makeup decisions to a flamboyantly gay Haitian called François. The style that year was to have one's hair "long and untamed," so, on François' recommendation, she had adopted a hairdo that was so wild it seemed vicious. All the mousse and red highlights made her hair seem like some kind of diseased porcupine. Yet, it was the style, and she was pleased with her appearance as she stared at her reflection.

When she walked into the bookstore there was a smile on her face, because there were at least two dozen people there, waiting for her to sign copies of her book, *How to Have Great Sex with a So-So Man*. On the cover there was a picture of a beaming woman standing next to a slouching doofus. The bookstore patrons froze and stared at her when she entered; some pointed to her and whispered to their neighbors, as if in awe of her. A couple of them snapped pictures of her, or began to record on their camcorders. Whatever the case, the mass of them moved toward her and put out their hands to be shaken. Soon there was a line to shake hands with her. Of course, all of them were women. Vera shook their hands gladly, smiling at each one and thanking her for coming. The store manager was a bookish-looking woman in her late-twenties: gaunt and severe-looking, with a sarcastic look pasted on her face from years of suppressing her disappointment with life.

"Let Dr. Vera get set-up first!" she chastised the patrons like a kindergarten teacher telling two five-year-olds to stop pulling one another's hair. Some of them groaned in disappointment, but Dr. Vera nodded to them, as if to reassure them that she would shake their hands later. They made room for her to pass, and she walked over to the desk where she was to sign books. A line had already formed; two women tussled with one another in their desire to occupy the same spot on the line. The store manager gave them her stern kindergarten teacher look and they calmed down.

Vera smiled at it all. She got out her fountain pen and sat down at the desk. Soon, she was asking the women their names and writing the same message in their books. She had developed a bad habit of writing and looking up at the person she was signing the book to. As a consequence, the message she wrote was usually illegible. Many people later discovered that she had misspelled their names, or she had written it merely as a line with a squiggly thing in the middle.

She had a good tempo going. In fifteen seconds, she could sign a book, dispense advice on the mysteries of male sexuality and still have time to pose for a picture. Even the sarcastic-looking store manager seemed impressed. The woman did not exactly smile, but she exuded a kind of pleased smugness as she stood to the side, surveying the long line.

"…Exactly," Vera said in answer to one woman's declaration of gratitude, "if you can teach a dog to shit outside, why can't teach your man to please you in bed!"

Everyone in the store laughed; some of them applauded. Vera had used that line about eighty times since she started her book tour a month ago. She had had a dream once, where it had been the only thing she could say...but people loved it when she said it.

She nodded to the woman who had made the declaration of gratitude (as to dismiss her) and the next woman on line stepped up to the table. People were still laughing at Vera's joke. However, the woman who stepped up to the table had a drawn, wretched expression on her face—like in those pictures of war refugees who had watched their children starve to death and their men butchered. The woman seemed about Vera's age, but could have possibly been about ten years older. With her thinness, the woman seemed frail and detached—except for the intensity with which she stared at Vera. It was off-putting, and Vera instinctively looked away. She noticed the woman's blouse: the nape of the neck was slightly frayed and discolored. Vera noticed a peculiar birthmark on the woman's neck. It was heart-shaped with a jagged line through it—a broken heart. The store manager looked at the woman disapprovingly, wondering if she could afford the $21 price of the book.

The woman handed Vera the book to sign, and Vera came back to her senses. She tried to reassure herself by smiling. "To whom am I signing this?" she said.

The woman's voice was low and ominous: "Don't pretend that you don't know me."

Vera's smile disappeared; all the background conversation in the store seemed to cease. "I'm sorry," Vera said, flustered, "...I don't—"

"Don't you *dare* pretend—*you* of all people!"

"I'm not—"

"I took the weight for you," the woman went on, suddenly animated. "I carried it while you were doing all this," she said, looking around the bookstore, as if all of it were Vera's and the woman's sacrifice had allowed her to attain it. "—But when is it going to be my turn to be free?" the woman lamented. "...The things we did," she said, beginning to sob, "—they're *killing* me—the weight of it all...! I can't take it anymore—it's too much for me."

Vera had sat stunned for most of that; the store patrons had stood staring. Vera remembered that she was a psychologist and stood up, to calm the woman. "Please—"

"I've lost everything," the woman cut her off, talking more to herself now than anything.

"Ma'am, please—"

"*Ma'am*?" she screamed, outraged by the formality and coldness of the term. "—After *all* we went through—all those things we did…?"

The store manager came over, but Vera warded her off by shaking her head. Vera walked around to the front of the desk and tried to take the woman's hand.

"No!" the woman screamed, as if brushing off a lover's hand. And then, more calmly, "If you don't remember me, it's too late for that. …It's too late." Her eyes were full of sorrow and desperation now: "…You were all I had left."

"Maybe you should sit down," Vera attempted to reason with her once more. She again tried to take the woman's hand, but the woman pushed her hand away. And then, with a disillusioned expression on her face:

"You *really* don't know me…?" She stared at Vera's face, as if searching for some clue of recognition; but seeing none, she bowed her head thoughtfully and started talking to herself again: "…I guess it's best that you forgot. I took the weight for you, but it's too much."

"Let's talk about it," Vera said, trying to think up every therapist trick she knew. "Maybe you can help me to remember."

The woman started to walk away, as if she had not heard.

"Please," Vera called after her, "—at least tell me your name!"

The woman stopped and stared at her as if considering something. At last she sighed, saying, "I'm the one who helped you to forget." At that, she walked out of the store. When she got to the curb, she looked back at Vera via the display window; then, she turned and took a step into the street. The speeding truck hit her instantly. She was sent flying like a cartoon character. There was something unbelievable about it—like a cheap special effect in a bad movie. The truck tried to stop, but the woman's careening body fell right in its path. There was the sound of tires screeching, and then a thud…and then silence.

F or Dr. Vera, four years passed in a blur of success and controversy. As was usually the case, the controversy had fueled her success. The entire episode with the woman at the bookstore had been captured on some of her fans' camcorders. The story got international attention. People called it "The Forget-Me-Not" incident, because of the woman's rant on being forgotten. A couple of networks did exposés on Dr. Vera, trying to figure out the connection between her and the woman: if there really was some deep dark secret that they had shared…but there had been nothing. The woman had spent her entire life in a small town in North Carolina; she had had a history of mental illness and had been living with a family friend until she snuck away to come to New York the day before she died. With all the media attention, the camcorder scenes of Dr. Vera attempting to calm the deranged woman had made her seem compassionate and accessible; and within weeks of the incident, Dr. Vera had been approached to do her own radio call-in show.

Four years later, the Dr. Vera radio call-in show was not exactly a hit, but it was broadcast nationwide, and there was talk of a television version. Since the incident, her agent had been telling her how she was on the verge of greatness. Her last book, *10 Steps to Find Out if Your Man is a Cheating Bastard* had been a number one bestseller…but that was two years ago, and she could not help thinking that her career was languishing.

As for her personal life, despite the fact that she was a relationship counselor, she was single and childless. It had been over a year since she had had sex, and the more she thought about it, the more certain she was that the young stud her agent had set her up with the last time had faked his orgasm just so he could get away from her! In bed, she seemed almost mouse-like—nothing like the voracious sexual beast she wrote about in her books. In college, two of her lovers had fallen asleep while making love to her. Granted, they had both been drunk at the time, but it had all set off a lifelong sense of sexual inadequacy—which was probably why she connected so well with her legion of fans. She knew how they wanted to feel about their sexuality, because she wanted the same feeling—the same fantasy. Her greatest fear was that people would discover she was lousy in bed. To a certain degree, she remained single because she was afraid one of her ex-boyfriends would write one of those tell-all books on her, cataloguing the horrific boredom of her sex. Every lover was a potential blackmailer.

...And if all that were not bad enough, she was growing tired of being Dr. Vera. Her last name was actually Alexander, not Vera, but it had become an accepted practice for media doctors to go by their first names—like Dr. Phil and Dr. Ruth—as to give a false sense of intimacy to their fans. Being Dr. Vera required vast amounts of energy—as was usually the case when one lived a lie. Every day, she told lies about lovers who were a figment of her imagination; she dispensed sexual advice on things that she, herself, was terrified to try. And with each passing day, it became clearer to her that she *hated* doing her call-in show. Five nights a week, it was the same tedious nonsense: women calling up to find out why their husbands or boy-friends did not love them anymore; people trying to manipulate their lovers into doing something (stupid), or who were merely calling to hear a psychological professional justify their scummy behavior. She knew that something would have to change soon or she would crack. Every once in a while she would have a nightmare where she failed totally at this life and again had to return to being a high school guidance counselor. The nightmare would motivate her to work harder for a few weeks, until she again felt herself on the verge of cracking.

"...Okay," Dr. Vera said after she had finished answering the last caller's question, "—we have time for one more call." She looked at the computer screen before her to see which caller was to be next, and then she pressed a button: "Matt from Minneapolis, how may I help you today?"

"Thanks for taking my call, Dr. Vera. I'm a longtime listener and first time caller." The man's chipper, excited voice annoyed her for some reason, but she retreated into her usual radio routine:

"Thank you, Matt. How may I help you today?"

"Well, Dr. Vera," Matt began, "I've come to the conclusion that I'm a lesbian."

"...Aren't you a man?" she asked, frowning at the computer screen.

"Yes."

Dr. Vera frowned deeper, and looked through the soundproof glass, at the engineer/producer. When she made eye contact with the huge, wooly-mammoth-looking man, he shrugged and bit into a gigantic submarine sandwich. Vera sighed and stared at the computer screen again, as if the answer to everything lay within it. She had trained herself to always give kind, considerate responses—even to the stupidest questions—but all she could think to say was, "Look, Matt, to be a lesbian, you sort of have to be a woman."

"That's a pretty sexist view!"

"How is that sexist?"

"It's sexist to believe that a man can't be a lesbian, just as it would be sexist to believe that a woman can't be an astronaut, or have her own radio call-in show."

Dr. Vera shook her head: "To be a lesbian, you have to be a woman," she maintained.

"Not at all: a lesbian is simply someone who wants to have sex with a lesbian."

"So, if I had sex with you, I'd be a lesbian?"

"Of course!"

Dr. Vera groaned, despite her usual attempt to maintain a professional/unflappable radio persona. Maybe it was the fact that it was Friday night and she wanted to go home. She wanted to get away from people and their sexual problems—at least for the weekend—

"Anyway," she said to move things along, "you think you're a lesbian trapped in a man's body?"

"Not at all—I'm secure in my lesbian-ness," he said, making up his own terms.

A side of Dr. Vera wanted to say something sarcastic like, "Good for you, girlfriend!" Instead, she sighed and said, "So what is your problem then?"

"Oh," Matt said, as if he'd forgotten, "...you see, the problem is that my boyfriend doesn't want to be a lesbian."

Dr. Vera hung up the phone and sighed. The theme music began to play in the background, and she glared at the producer as if to say, *Aren't you supposed to be screening these calls!* However, he was too busy devouring his sandwich to notice her. "Cherished friends," she began her usual sign-off message without enthusiasm, "this brings us to the conclusion of another wonderful show. This is Dr. Vera, reminding you that every day can be a great day if you choose to see it that way. Until next time, my friends...!"

As soon as she was off the air she groaned again, grabbed her huge handbag and walked out of the studio. The summer night was hot and humid. The studio was in midtown Manhattan; when Vera got outside, there were thousands of teenagers milling about on the sidewalk. A rock star named Pastranzo had done an interview at the station about four hours ago, when Vera was coming in to work. Awestruck teenage girls had screamed and passed out at the prospect of meeting their hero; ambulances and huge phalanxes of police officers had had to be called in to quell the hysteria. The worst of it seemed to be over, but even though Pastranzo had left the studio hours ago (through a side entrance) the teenagers refused to believe it. They stood their ground, baking in the summer heat with the crazed obstinacy of goats. Vera, who had had to fight her way through the crowd when coming into work, was now forced to do the same thing upon leaving.

All of a sudden, a squealing 14-year-old ran up to her with arms open wide, perhaps thinking that Vera was Pastranzo. As Vera did not have the patience to explain the difference between herself and a stringy-haired Italian man, she put some sense into the girl's head the most efficient way she knew: with a firm backhand.

When she got to the curb, she hailed a cab and headed to Brooklyn. The cab smelled of vomit, curry and toe jam, so she opened the window and groaned again as she sat there brooding.